# DIARY OF AN ANT

*Eleven (mainly) Dark Yarns from the Irish Gaelic*

## Tomás Mac Síomóin

NUASCÉALTA

# DIARY OF AN ANT

# CONTENTS

# ACKNOWLEDGMENTS

I would like to express my profound gratitude to Hazel Ní Mhaoláin for her assistance in preparing translations into English of the stories from Cín Lae Seangáin and for having the forbearance to entertain my views on her efforts, especially at those times we failed to see eye-to-eye.

My thanks to Pádraig Ó Snodaigh, Coiscéim Teoranta, who took the risk of publishing the original Gaelic version of these stories, and to Aindrias Ó Cathasaigh for having edited them.

Finally, but by no means least, my great appreciation to the dedicated editorial work of Robert Edelstein for Nuascéalta Teoranta.

Go mba fada buan sibh uilig!


Tomás Mac Síomóin
Sant Feliu de Guíxols, Catalunya
Eanáir, 2013

# PREFACE

That Irish Gaelic literary culture adopted the short story as its flagship form is hardly surprising as it is but a short jump from a rich oral storytelling tradition as old as the Gaelic language itself. In Ireland, Pádraig Ó Conaire and Seosamh Mac Grianna pioneered that jump in early 20th century. Following mid-century masters of the form such as Máirtín Ó Cadhain, Diarmuid Ó Súilleabháin, and Liam Ó Flaithearta (Liam O'Flaherty) a plethora of innovative successors have arrived who have generated an exciting body of highly innovative and quintessentially modern writing. Better known as a prize-winning poet and novelist, Tomás Mac Síomóin belongs to this movement.

The stories of *Diary of an Ant* take a darkly humorous look at the failure of human emotional interaction, vitiated by an overwhelming need to conform to herd norms in a milieu where self-interest is the paramount value. Thus, in *Julieta*, the attempt of the "hero" to construct an "ideal" woman in accordance with mainline male fantasy, can be read as a fictionalized neo-feminist tract in which male chauvinist arrogance reaps its merited come-uppance. *Birth* joins and divides the Anglo-Irish colonizer and the Gaelic colonized in mutual incomprehension; marital relations are corroded by dishonesty in *Saké is the Divil* and *Sean-Nós* alloys destiny with moral cowardice. The protagonists of his Belfast story, *When the Batteries Give Out*, find their after-death conversations to be the same inconsequentialities as those in which they engaged before being effaced by the armed struggle. *A Warning to Our Neighbors* sees the Greed-is-Good consumerist dispensation and the class tensions that simmer beneath its "civilized" façade morph into dehumanization and savagery. The underbelly of Celtic Tiger Ireland is depicted brutally in an ironically named bar, *Last Order in the Celtic Tradition*. The espousing of neoliberal values lead to the ultimate irremediable alienation in *The Diary of an Ant*. Retention of Gaelic references in the translation will give the reader some flavor of the originals.

These stories defy easy labeling. Mac Síomóin's frequent use of surprising and surreal imagery has invited the sobriquet of magical realism. They can also be classified as black humor, speculative or dark fiction.

English-language literary culture in contemporary Ireland, largely frozen in a posture of neocolonial cultural cringe, ignores, with few exceptions, the vibrant, innovative tradition to which *Diary of an Ant* belongs. These translations will serve, hopefully, to draw attention to this highly developed but sadly neglected sector of the European short story tradition.

Hazel Ní Mhaoláin
Salem, Massachusetts
19 October 2012

*Men of broader intellect know that there is no sharp distinction betwixt the real and the unreal...*
H.P. Lovecraft , *The Tomb*

# JULIETA

**IT WAS ONLY A FEW DAYS** after Ann died, may the good Lord be merciful to her, that an envelope with a strange logo incorporating the words Marital Electronics Ltd arrived in my letterbox. I had so many duties to fulfill at that time—funeral costs to estimate, Ann's boozy western relatives to send home  (they being enthusiastically disposed to prolong the wake indefinitely), thank-you notes to dispatch to the senders of Mass cards etc.—that I placed that envelope in a drawer for later consideration. And completely forgot about it.

After a year of my unexpected widowhood, an interval of chastity lived out of respect for the dead, certain basic needs that require a woman for their complete fulfillment made their presence felt in both body and soul. And that fulfillment was nowhere in sight, discounting the usual commercial outlets. When the good Saint Paul spoke of 'the thorn in the flesh', that blessed boyo surely knew what he was talking about.

It was at that time that the kindly Fates, may they be thrice blessed (or so I prayed at that time), paid heed to my plight. I was rummaging in a drawer in the kitchen for the Phillips screwdriver that vanishes mysteriously when need for it is the greatest.

Unexpectedly, I caught sight there of that forgotten envelope with its curiously ambiguous Marital Electronics Ltd. logo. I opened it hurriedly and read the following communication:

*Dear Bartholomew,*

*Our sincerest sympathies on the recent death of your beloved wife, Ann. We understand fully the emptiness that the loss of an affectionate life-long partner has left in your life—a loss that can never be fully made good. For nothing under the sun can replace the affection of a loving wife.*

*But there is something practical you can do to console yourself and to replace, at least partly, an important aspect of your shared life together.The product we are offering you, Julieta, is a stunningly beautiful, flexible, soft flesh-colored life sized (170cm) and totally realistic electronic woman who reacts instinctively to your caresses. Incorporating the latest in electronic and materials technology, Julieta has a perfect full female figure, with long shapely legs and erectile nipples. When connected to the mains or portable battery (also available directly from us at Marital Electronics Ltd.), Juliet's skin temperature (27 C) and skin-feel factor are identical to those of a living woman, and she is programmed to emit life-like sighs and whimpers of pleasure at the appropriate moments.*

*And can she ever talk! Juliet comes with an incorporated state-of-the-art digital file that gives her over 200 spicy pillow-talk options in all EU official languages (plus Mandarin) to whisper into your ear. Also, she comes with a stunning range of sexy lingerie and negligees.*

*Julieta will not only be your kissable huggable electronic lover but—with 7 beautiful easily detachable heads (and more on demand), she will be a different wife every night—a guaranteed lifelong electronic harem to satisfy every man's secret dream!*

*We hesitate to intrude on your privacy, but even at this sorrowful moment in your life the future beckons. And for €10,000, our unrepeatable price offer, Juliet can help you to leave a heartbreaking past behind and make the brightest of bright new futures possible.*

*Please do not hesitate to contact us, at your convenience, if we can be of assistance. Additional information concerning the services we offer is available at our website. Once again, be assured that your sorrow is our sorrow.*

*Sincerely,*

*Jason X. Haughey Jr.*
*Director,International Sales Division*
*Marital Electronics PLC*

How the hell did this gang access my name and address? I ask myself. From the deaths column in the local newspaper of course! The envelope also contained a glossy full-color brochure with photographs demonstrating the multifaceted charms of the Marital Electronics harem I was now being offered. From a cursory look, I instantly recognized from my newspaper gleanings most of the damsels on display. Marilyn Monroe was there of course, Lady Di and Madonna... but can this be, somewhat improbably, among such a gaggle of pop celebrities, Margaret Thatcher, albeit in her heyday? Yes, the head of the former British Prime Minister sits there, somewhat incongruously, on Juliet's lush body, clothed in a skimpy negligee that reveals much more tantalizing, albeit plastic, flesh than it conceals. And more! Given that her picture is at least three times the size of her fellow nymphs, Angela Merkel would appear to be queen of Marital Electronics harem. I search the folder in vain for Sophia Loren, erotic idol of my misspent youth... But who, in the name of Almighty Crom[1], is this? Why, it can be none other than Mary Robinson, ex-President of Ireland and ex-United Nations Commissioner for Human Rights. We are here in exalted company indeed, and Juliet's minimalist wisp of a bikini so well becomes that much-travelled lady. I feel myself at liberty to disclose

---

[1]  *Chief god of an Irish Gaelic pagan pantheon.*

here that, apart from Kim Kardashian and Megan Fox who also figure in Marital Electronics' current galaxy of stars, a cursory browsing of www.passionsolutions.com affords the lover a much wider range of fantasy partners "from the worlds of celebrities and power, to classic sultry celluloid goddesses": Hillary Clinton, Marlene Dietrich, Oprah Winfrey ("with Afro-American body"), Cristina Fernández Kirchner, Melina Mercouri, Elizabeth Windsor (crown included), Rita Hayward, Christine Lagarde, Elizabeth Taylor, among many others...

I must say that the contents of this Marital Electronics' communiqué occasioned in me, at first, an uncontrollable bout of hilarity. Imagine love's sweet dalliance about to reach its ethereal culmination just as the Electricity Supply Board's operatives commence their walk-out strike. Or that the master fuse goes bang, and Ms. Juliet's sexy murmurings (in fluent Mandarin) cease accordingly, at the appropriate moment, as Marital Electronics so delicately describes that pinnacle of all human erotic endeavor. However, loneliness does the strangest things to the mind of man. And, when my hilarity subsided, I found myself weighing up the pros and cons of having an electronic lady share my living space.

For starters, Juliet would come to me totally free of ideological, or any other, baggage. Nor would she ever pester me with stupid stories about celebrities, famous for being famous. The to-ings and fro-ings of parasitic European royalty and sundry snazzily-suited sociopathic celebrities need never again assault my ears. Nor need I ever again cast my opinions regarding the future of the planet (bleak), the failure of capitalism (inevitable and long-predicted), psychology (Fraud and Junk) postmodernist philosophy (smoke and mirrors) or Barcelona Football Club (messy without Messi?), before the indifferent snout of some intellectually non-reflective creature. Sorry about that, Ann, as you lie there in your cold grave, but the truth is often bitter. And home truths the bitterest of all!

But what would the neighbors think?

Let me make myself very clear! I, Bartholomew B., a 21st century broad-minded European, couldn't give two buttons about the opinions of those mean-spirited *untermenschen*, my neighbors, whose herd-script is, to him (me), total anathema. Nevertheless, living as I do in a land of squinting windows, I had needs be resourceful and crafty. And all the more so, given that I am a teacher, forever in the public view and with a responsible public position. One always has to take into account the school Principal, that creep, stinking of cheap cigars, who devotes more time to playing the horses than to his administrative duties. Not to mention the Board of Management (gregarious gaggle of headless geese). Nor does one forget the students, that pimpled rabble! How would all of these insects who people Bartholomew B's universe react in if they found out that the, for all intents and purposes, their "normal" Bartholomew B. was covertly co-inhabiting with, and enjoying the charms of, Miss Monroe, Hillary, Angela, Mary and all the rest of Marital Electronics' glittering harem. Nor should I care to be privy to the inevitably corrosive comments that would be made in the Teacher's Common Room.

Morality?

Do you really think that I was born yesterday? If you don't realize by now, dear reader, that morality is constituted of eyes, ears, mouths—and, if needs be—of burning torches and pitchforks, I do not envy your sheep-like innocence. However, in a little cynical aside, let us focus on what has replaced your notional "morality" in this present unblessed epoch of the unfettered market: MONEY, and the mindset that engenders obsession with same, that has largely replaced what was once known as morality! As Doña Maria José makes so abundantly clear, as she spits out her reiterated "*Es la Venganza de Mamón!*"[2] in Rodriguez Perreira's little-known similarly

---

[2] "*It's the Revenge of Mammon!*"

titled send-up of her (and our) times. So, in that spirit, let's get on with it:

Ann stuck me for a basic €60 every week, food, drinks and weekend entertainment included. But, of course, realistically, that was only the beginning. For she was, may God in his infinite mercy be good to her, very heavy on the fags, just one example of her extramural expenditures. Those horribly pungent smelling Gauloises destroyed her lungs in the end, apart from rendering our sitting room well-nigh uninhabitable). Without mentioning her other extravagances (a post mortem sight that took me aback was the huge army of sherry bottles, in their primal state of chaotic disorder, stashed in the cupboard underneath the stairs). So, it was abundantly obvious that a new wife would cost me €5000, at least, per annum. One could anticipate this expenditure rising year by year, depending on the extravagances such creatures are always bound to cultivate: €8000, €12,000, €16,000...and inflation has not even entered into this calculation.

But, as regards Julieta, I would be stung for a once off payment of €10,000 only. And from there on out, given that electronic lovers like her neither eat nor drink, our life together would cost me nothing extra, excepting a tiny increase in my electricity bill (the internet informs me that electronic equipment is highly power-efficient). The only drawback in selecting Julieta rather than a flesh and blood spouse would be my ineligibility for a Marriage Allowance. But, as between having Julieta or a living spouse as life partner, rather than any of the bright-eyed would-be brides I had met by virtue of my membership of the Cupid Club (the online dating service for the "seriously matrimonially inclined") a distinct economic advantage would be with the former arrangement!

However, all things considered, it was not a decision to be taken lightly. So, I weighed the pros and cons of the situation interminably for a good half year. My stance during this period reminded me of Búradán's celebrated ass, who could not decide which of the two carrots in front of him he was going to eat and who died from hunger because he was incapable of making a choice. Nor was I getting any younger and I sensed Sonny Boy Death—a palpable physical presence there in my wristwatch—giving silent voice to his somber countdown! Thence, one fine day, throwing patience and reason to the winds, I made the great decision. Please do not ask me why I opted for Julieta. The reasons of the heart are seldom, if ever, founded on pure reason, though the subliminal relevance of the economic factor can never be discounted.

As it happens, said the brisk no-nonsense voice of the Marital Electronics marketing lady, a new consignment of Julietas has just arrived... the very latest model, but I advise you to hurry up; they are already in great demand. You will really like her. All you have to do is to launch a deposit of €300 in our account (if you have a pencil handy, I'll give you the details), the balance to be paid when Julieta arrives on your doorstep, all ready for action (followed by a lecherous chuckle), within about a fortnight.

Like a man hypnotized, I fulfilled the conditions laid down by Ms. Briskvoice. Once that die was cast, a stranger fortnight I have never spent. I sensed a strange rogue *kundalini*, as it were, pulsing within me. I scrubbed the house from top to bottom, tidied up the garden (which had seen neither rake nor lawnmower since Ann had passed away) and brushed the walls of my (soon to be our) bedroom with a golden ochre paint. If that were not enough, I bought a couple of new suits in one of the more up-market tailoring establishments in the city together with a brace of white shirts and two pairs of shoes. I bundled my old suits and shirts into a black plastic garbage sack which I bequeathed to the local charity shop.

A fortnight does not correspond always to two weeks on my native heath. But, as a consequence of the many phone calls I made to Ms. Briskvoice (who doesn't answer e-mails and whose tone of voice indicated that she was gradually losing patience with me) my doorbell rang with a timbre that presaged the end of my fevered wait. Krupp Delivery ("Delivery in a Day-the Kaydee Way") had indeed arrived with Julieta in a large box under plain cover.

As the box was indeed as heavy as it looked, the burly delivery man himself kindly offered to place it in the house, anywhere I wished. I chose the dining room. Huffing and puffing, he hefted the box to the place I showed him.

Looking quizzically then at the candelabra and the bottle of champagne reclining in its ice bucket and the table set for two, Mr. Kaydee asked: 'Are you expecting visitors here tonight?'

'No... I mean I am!' I answered somewhat confusedly. That's it: a visitor, as you say yourself. You can put the box down there, I said, indicating a spot beside the chair at the head of the table.

Now, sir, if you could sign on the dotted line here, said Mr. Kaydee, the ash from his cigarette falling on my new carpet. As I scribbled my signature on the docket with a trembling hand, he reminded me of the balance that is owing to Marital Electronics, sir; that will be €2700.

Don't worry; I have it here...Just look at the check in this envelope to make sure I am not leaving you short, I say. And here is something for you! I pushed a €20 note into his far from unwilling fist.

Thank you very much, sir. Here it is the receipt and I hope that you get a lot of pleasure from, well... her, you know what I mean... his words trailed off as he looked in the direction of the box. And then he winked at me. A long lewd wink! The bastard! A knowing mocking look dancing in his other eye! Such an appalling lack of taste and civilized empathy after he had soiled my new carpet with cigarette ash and my nuptial largesse had left him €20 the richer!

When I slammed the door after the Kaydee barbarian withdrew, I swallowed a deep breath and poured out a generous glass of Redbreast whiskey for myself to temper the rising frenzy, (the word is not excessive!) within me. Mendelssohn's Wedding March was beginning to gather intensity on the edge of my consciousness, as the recently arrived box became the cynosure of my ardent gaze.

For the time has come, my Sleeping Beauty, to release you from the claustrophobic confines of your cardboard prison and to let your beauty illuminate and heat with conjugal warmth the monastic bleakness of this bachelor's quarters!

As I tore frantically at the box, my hands shaking with excitement, the spectacular images of Julieta, as she is represented in the Marital Electronics website, flashed provocatively across the screen of my imagination. O slender goddess, o vestal virgin, o flower of womanhood, now to be released from your dark prison to savor the bright light of freedom! Soon my hand, empowered by love, will be stroking your brow of the purest marble, your snow-soft breast. But, fuck it all to hell, this box is so trussed up with masking tape that a sharp knife will be needed to open it.

However, my carving knife makes short work of the masking tape and I tear once again at the box again with my bare hands. Something is coming into sight. But what, in God's name, can it be?

Styrofoam! Yes, blocks of Styrofoam, neatly packed. I removed one such block from the package and turned it over. Ugh! The thing embedded in this block almost makes me throw up. A human hand! So realistic that I had to persuade myself that it was made of plastic. I picked another block out of the package. Yuk! An ear this time, just as realistic as the hand, with electrical wiring trailing from it...

Bloody hell! What Marital Electronics has sent me is a DIY

kit, with Julieta as the item to be assembled. So much for their ready-for-action propaganda! What was to be a festive marriage feast now lay in ruins. I retired to the side board and poured myself another generous glass of Redbreast, to somehow preserve my sanity and lower my resistance to facing the mammoth assembly task in front of me. For it seems that my bride has arrived in hundreds, if not thousands, of bits.

One hour later and my sitting room resembled nothing so much as the kitchen of a cannibalistic serial killer. Lifelike (if I didn't know any better) blue eyes and brown eyes stared glassily at me from their Styrofoam beds! Hands here, a thigh there, a foot stands incongruously on a ribcage. Juliet's trunk standing on the dining table, needed to be hidden by the appropriate piece of lingerie. Otherwise her breasts would resemble jellyfish stranded on ocean beaches, not the most erotically arousing sight ever known to man. Shining bald heads abound; it seems that the appropriate wigs have to be affixed to them with gum, a huge tube of which (presumably for that purpose) lay there on the floor. The sight might have excited Madame Defarge, knitting away there in the shadow of the guillotine, but it left Bartholomew B. cold. Beside them, also laid out on the table, was a somewhat intricate apparatus seemingly related to that "appropriate moment", as mentioned coyly in Marital Electronics' propaganda! But who knows! Julieta/Hillary seemed to be eyeing me (hardly *le mot juste*) through empty sockets from her/their perch on top of the television set.

The aspect of all of this mess that genuinely horrified me, however, is that complicated tangle of wires and electronic components that I have unboxed—Julieta's neurological wiring, so to speak—an aspect of her anatomy, apart from electronics per se, about which I know absolutely nothing. How, I asked myself, in the name of Crom Almighty, am I going to assemble such a confusing *gemisch*?

One day later, and still parked on the horns of a dilemma, I espied a gleam of light amongst the Styrofoam rubble. In the form of *The Julieta Doll Assembly Kit Manual*! Like the original brochure, it is a lush technicolored production. In a pocket inside the back cover I detected a map that I instantly extracted and spread out on the table in front of me. A not so muted black night of the soul descended upon me as I surveyed, with mounting dismay, the convoluted assemblage of electrical connections here, electrical connections there, that constituted the neurological apparatus of my much fragmented electronic bride. Poets like me are not exactly the most practical people on this doomed planet. Even in my former state of wedded unbliss, Ann was the one who changed the light bulbs. However, I told myself, my limited childhood exposure to Lego and Meccano assembly kits should, at least, help me to accomplish a successful reconstruction of Julieta. In her purely anatomical aspect, at least.

Things, alas, are never as simple as what, at first, they seem. For, according to my recently discovered instruction manual (Section 5, p. 3), if I had understood these instructions correctly (not at all an easy exercise), the would-be assembler was warned that both corporeal and neurological component integration must be conducted in tandem. In tandem, for Crom's sake! However, balking at such confusion will not complete this task, I told myself! I poured myself another stiff whisky and headed, with colors flying and pipes blaring, into the heat of battle.

Four hours later, I understood, ruefully, that this task was away more complicated than I has at first imagined. I did manage to attach one arm to Julieta's trunk, fair dues to me, before discovering that it should have been attached to the opposite side of her upper thorax. The form of the top of her thigh didn't correspond in any meaningful way to that the slot at the base of her thorax which is, according to the manual, supposed to receive it. None of the heads could be attached to the trunk, via her detachable neck, without first installing Juliet's obscenely complex neurological network.

I was utterly flummoxed upon discovering that I was unable to distinguish between the various unlabeled electronic components, each of which has its own unique function to fulfill in a fully operational Julieta. A warning in heavy red print informed me that incorrect placing of any of these components can 'permanently blow Juliet's mind' (*sic*). I drained the dregs left in the bottom of the whiskey bottle and retired, precipitously and with lowered colors, drums beating the retreat, from the field of battle.

On the midnight hour, having disassembled the laughably little of Julieta I had managed to put together, I began to review the progress of the campaign. The first glaringly obvious conclusion was that much more time than I anticipated would be required to fully assemble Julieta. And that a fresh beginning, with a clear head, was plainly needed if I was to come to grips successfully with the daunting task in front of me.

Resolution: I shall arise early tomorrow morning and call the school to inform them that I am sick. And then spend the entire day assembling Julieta. Firm in this resolve, I take to my bed. Before the arrival of the Sandman, I see the many faces of Juliet, alternatively mocking and flirting with me. You just wait, bitch, I said; if other people have put you together, so can I!

I was wrong! Four days later I had to admit that the realization of the dream is as far away from me now as it ever was. And that many of the technical problems that emerged in the course of the work appeared to be insoluble.

To give a few examples (and one could add substantially to this list): (1) it seems that my many efforts to join the left thigh to the thorax has resulted in a small amount of damage to both aforesaid parts so that they are no longer structurally reconcilable. (2) Having studied and restudied the appropriate section of the instruction manual, I still failed to see how Julieta's "reproductive" organs could be accommodated in the base of her thorax, given the complexity of the neurological map of this area of her anatomy. I had no idea as to what those stray wires trailing from the base of her clitoris were to be connected with, for example. (3) The efforts I made to assemble a complete nervous system of Julius outside her body, as advised in the instructions (Section 23, page 8) resulted in disaster. The latter word is not excessive. I might mention here that this instruction appeared to contradict Section 2, page 1. When I connected it— the nervous system—to the electricity mains, not only did the red light in the control unit fail to show up, as described in the manual, but nothing happened. For a few seconds, at least! And then, a small explosion in the component associated with the movement of Juliet's eyes (I think!) followed by a puff of nastily acrid smoke...

It then seemed to me that the instruction manual itself could very well have been at the heart of the problem. The text of the manual appeared to me to have been translated, word for word, from the original Japanese. When I was unable to make sense of the English language version, I tried to follow the German text with the help of Rundtscheidt's technical dictionary (Bad Wurttemberg, 2004). For all of the good that did me! The German instructions seemed to me to be nothing more, nor less, than a poor translation of the egregiously unintelligible English version. Unless of course they are not written in *Hochdeutsch* at all, but rather in medieval *Plattdeutsch* or some obscure variant of early Gothic, as once spoken in what is now present-day Poland!

Hello! Marital Electronics here. Can I help?

I am sorry to hear of the fix you find yourself in, Bartholomew B., says Ms. Briskvoice, but none of our other Romeos appear to have had the same problem as yours. Everybody else finds following the instructions in the manual to be mere child's play. Are you absolutely certain that you are following the steps laid out in the manual in the sequence Marital Electronics indicates?

In the imagination's eye, I saw those technophilic Romeos, thousands of them worldwide, each of them cuddling up to the 'soft, warm-skinned satin-smoothness' of his lovingly-assembled Julieta. My soul is convulsed for a moment by a spasm of jealousy.

I say: I can make neither head nor tail of your instructions; they are nothing but gibberish. I speak with a certain authority here as I can boast a first class honors English degree. So, dear, you are not talking to some lobotomized halfwit. I have spent four full days, working from morning till night, trying to assemble Juliet. I may do some irreparable damage to the kit, if I haven't done so already. Couldn't you to send somebody who understands how to assemble Julieta out to me?

We don't have anybody of that ilk on tap, sir. We don't manufacture Julieta; we just market and distribute her and related products. Technical help comes to us once or twice a year from Japan. As it so happens, Mr. Takahashi left Dublin yesterday; he should be in Khabarovsk by now. He had so little to do here this time as the Irish have become so *au fait* with technical matters, as he said himself. He is a lovely man, in his own way!.. He kept on saying that he really missed his sashimi. Although I'd say those creamy pints of Guinness made up for it to a certain extent. But for this hankering after sashimi, I mean, he could be just as Irish as you or I, you know what I mean. Now, if only you had spoken to us a few days ago... My own opinion, for what it is worth, is that you are trying to put Julieta together far too quickly. That happens sometimes when customers become over-excited. Remember that when God made time, he made lots of it. So, calm down, Bartholomew B! Courage and patience are the virtues you must cultivate. And stick to the instruction manual procedure. That is your golden rule. Follow the instructions to the letter.

This is all highly bloody unsatisfactory, I say. I need to speak directly to your Managing Director, or whoever is in charge of your set-up.

I am afraid that Mr. Haughey is at a meeting right now.

If Mohammed won't come to the mountain, then the mountain must come to Mohammed! Could you for God's sake give me your address!

No problem, Sir! You will find us at 214 Glenlongan Park. You cannot miss the blue and red neon sign with our company logo and there is always someone in the office between 9 and 5 PM. Mr. Haughey, Jason, is always here in the mornings. Would you like me to make an appointment for you with him for tomorrow morning, say?

When I find out later that 214 Glenlongan Park is a bogus address, I sense a gigantic bubble of laughter begin to grow within me. If one could refer to the barely perceptible giggle that first developed in my entrails, burgeoning and strengthening there without my being able to arrest its development. That explodes up my backbone, into my chest before reaching my vocal chords. That unites in the back of my throat with another lunatic current descending from my brain. A laugh that possesses me fully in both mind and body! That roars out of my mouth like an unstoppable flood tide, filling the sitting room, the house, the street, Dublin, Europe, the World, and the Universe.

Now I understand that this infinite guffaw underlies all that was, that is and will be. That great roaring guffaw of the Goddess for which I am and will ever be merely a vehicle, for that Joke of Jokes that has neither beginning nor end...

That ultimate joke that is always on you, Bartholomew B.!

# WHEN THE BATTERIES GIVE OUT

**ALIGHTING FROM THE BLACK TAXI** at the bottom of Falls Road, I walk briskly away from it into the smoggy Belfast dusk.

Big raindrops stream through the pale yellow light cast by the street lamps. I pull up my coat collar and shiver involuntarily. Weaving among the waves of oncoming pedestrians returning from work, I avoid having my eyes speared by their umbrellas of as they face into a chill north easterly.

My mood is hardly lifted by the gaudy Christmas lights and decorations in the windows of the small shops that line this shabby street. Grinning red-faced Santa Clauses and reindeer stand in white cotton wool snow. Red balloons abound. Overlie that tinsel gaiety with the background music of car horns, honking impatiently over in Royal Avenue, the city's main thoroughfare! Blend in the characteristic smell of this rust-belt industrial burg, its unique blend of noxious industrial fumes diluted by copious volumes of car exhaust—never incense in a countryman's nostrils—and there we have a sensory symphony that correlates exactly with my mood as I consider my present assignment.

Once again, I curse *sotto voce*, the editor who had condemned this particular reporter to cover the book launch to which I was now heading. However, there seemed to be little point now in protesting the decision of McCafferty, our editor almighty, to send me rather than Séamas Rafferty, a fluent Irish speaker and, hence, the logical choice for such an occasion. I tried to convince McCafferty that whatever knowledge of the Irish language I once possessed now lay moribund under many years of rust. To no avail! I then told him that the occasion itself was of little importance and hardly worthy of being recorded. Even Irish speakers no longer read books in their own language, I said.

Once again, to no avail!

And then, my argument of last resort, I reminded him that it was on the basis of my expert knowledge of international affairs that I had been employed by the *Northern Courier*. And that it ill behooved said journal to waste such a specialized talent on covering what was, when all is said and done, a minor parochial event.

However, Séamas Rafferty, the Courier's official Irish speaker had been sent up to Divis Flats to cover yet another demonstration against the British Army presence there, explained McCafferty.

Tough luck!

So that you, O'Rourke, are the only journalist available to me who is competent enough to cover this book launch in the Ulster Arms Hotel. As the event is to be conducted wholly through the beloved language of our forefathers, nobody else in the office but Rafferty and yourself would understand even half of what was being said there.

It seems the godly McCafferty is of the opinion that every Mayo man, like myself, is a fluent Irish speaker. But, in truth, I prefer to downplay my knowledge of the language to avoid being relegated to Peg's Corner, McCafferty's cynical designation of the small Irish-language section of the *Courier* in which social events related to the Irish language, and therefore of marginal interest, are sporadically recorded.

Let Rafferty, the language enthusiast, carry the can for that particular cause!

In any case, this event tonight is far from being simply much ado about nothing, as you seem to imagine, continues McCafferty. If you hailed from this neck of the woods, Mike, you would understand clearly that the public outings of the Cardinal are always news among our readers. And that for many of our middle-class readers' ecumenicism is the very much the flavor of the month... Also they expect to have some guest speakers from the South at that blessed book launch. So have 500 words on the happenings there ready for me before 10:30 p.m. And, if you please, no more fuckin arguments about it!

Once again, I damn whatever malign fate destined me to be employed by such a popehead journal as the *Northern Courier*!

Leaving the city center, I take a shortcut through the narrow talk streets of this nationalist ghetto. A patrol of British Army squaddies comes towards me, silent on its rubber-soled combat boots. Young pimply youths for the most part, their automatic rifles at the ready. Nothing unusual about this these days! They scan warily the dark entrance of every alleyway. Squint at imaginary snipers lurking behind unlit windows.

For this is *Injun* territory and we are at war to defend the Queen's writ in this troubled realm, as we have been doing for the last 400 years, against Her Majesty's Irish enemies! The soldiers leap lithely from shadow to shadow, never straying far from the comforting cover of walls. For all the world like space explorers investigating the empty plains of some foreign planet, an impression reinforced by those swaying aerials sticking up from their back packs.

A heavy explosion in the immediate vicinity awakens echoes on Divis Mountain, to the west of the city. The soldiers jump, visibly startled, and squat down immediately on their haunches in the shadow of a high wall. I hear the soldier who brought up the rear of the squad, a lithe and lanky young Negro, saying in his high-pitched Cockney voice:

*Tha' wuz a fuggin rocket, tha' wuz! It's gonna be one o' those fuggin nights, mytes.*

The words LOUGHGALL: PARAS 8, IRA 0 are scrawled, somewhat inelegantly, in red paint, high on an end-wall of a house in the Loyalist ghetto, which is clearly visible over the barrier that separates the warring tribes of Ulster, from where I stand.

It is answered triumphantly by a WARRENPOINT: IRA 18, PARAS 0 on the wall just above the crouching soldiers. Grim ledger of battle casualties in the latest chapter in this interminable war for which no definitive end appears to be in sight.

Another 10 minutes' walk from here should see me arriving at the Ulster Arms Hotel. It is now 5.30 p.m. and the launch is due to commence right now. Or is it to be at 6.30 p.m.? Too bad I didn't pay more attention to the green invitation card that McCafferty handed me before I left the office. It is too dark to read it here.

Out of the corner of my eye I notice a policeman, wearing his bulky flak jacket standing at the edge of the sidewalk looking up and down the street. A submachine gun lies in the crook of his arm and the black butt of a pistol juts out from its leather holster on his hip. The badge on his black peaked police cap shows the British crown sitting on an Irish harp.

I pause before a lighted shop window, more than usually ablaze with gaudy Christmas tinsel decorations, to examine my invitation card. The policeman turns around looking at me suspiciously from under the peak of his cap, placing his hand on the handgrip of his submachine gun. Letting the light from the window illuminate the invitation in my hand, I read, in Irish, the following:

*Reconciliation Limited*
*has the pleasure of inviting you to be present*
*at the Ulster Arms Hotel*
*on 20 October at 5:30 p.m.*
*when his Eminence, Cardinal Tomás Ó Fiaich will launch*
Gaelic Presbyterians of Fermanagh
*by Dr. Aodh Ó Cuinn, ME, PhD.*
*Drinks and refreshments will be available.*

I consult my watch. It is 5.45 p.m. I am already fifteen minutes late. I realize, of course, that 5.30 p.m. in Belfast is code for 6.00 p.m. Still, I had better get a move on. Just in case the unexpected happens and the occasion starts on the designated hour. But as I begin to walk ahead, the policeman calls me, his submachine gun pointing in my direction. In times such as these, discretion is the better part of valor!

Come here, he says, in an almost angry voice that nearly conceals his jumpiness. Who are you? And what are you doing nosing around here?

I note his strong Derry accent or, more likely, that of loyalist Waterside, Londonderry. I calmly return the hostile stare of this doughty defender of law and order in the full confidence that my press card and the invitation in my pocket will adequately explain my presence here at this time.

I am a reporter with the *Belfast Courier*. Right now, I am on my way to the Ulster Arms Hotel to make a report on an event that is being held there.

Have you got your press card, then? the machinegun toter asks. Somewhat brusquely, perhaps put on alert by my Southern accent.

I extract the magical invitation from my pocket and extend it, together with the press card, towards him. He looks at the press card first, and grunts affirmatively before squinting screw-eyed at my invitation to the book launch.

What in the name of God is this supposed to be? Is it written in some weird leprechaun language?

It is an invitation to a book launch and it is written in the Irish language, I say, somewhat dryly.

Wisdom gleaned from the practice of my profession in this neck of the woods dictates that, at best, it would be folly and a total waste of time to antagonize such an adversary as this. Or to respond in kind to his sarcasm! His eyes narrow as he surveys my name, particularly my surname. Certain Os and Macs are usually dead giveaways when the ethnic origins of the holders of such surnames are in question.

You must be some sort of leprechaun yourself then, he says, laughing heartily at his own somewhat feeble wit. It strikes me then that this policeman is attempting, in his own clumsy way, to be friendly. You find lobsters in the strangest places, as they say in Irish. His genial ignorance does not enable him, however, to recognize his humor as the insult that it, in fact, it is to its recipient.

All of your crowd should understand, (placing a particular emphasis on the words "your crowd")—especially journalists—that is not advisable to be hanging around this area at this time. This is no man's land, after all, where anything can—and often does—happen! And after that slaughter last night in the Rangers bar, certain persons who hang out not far from here will be dead set on revenge. I think that your own newspaper published this morning that warning statement from the UDA! It is for your own good that I am telling you this.

I thank the RUC man for his solicitude.

The girl at the reception desk in the Ulster Arms Hotel is examining her nails when I reach the hotel. They are long and pointed and as red as blood. Hardly looking up at me, she says in a bored voice:

If it's the Irish crowd you're looking for, you'll find them down there in the Events Room at the then returns to the real business of inspecting her nails.

After walking down the thickly-carpeted corridor on silent feet, I reach a closed door bearing a placard with the following message in bold print:

**SEOLADH LEABHAIR**

*IRISH BOOK LAUNCH*

Journey's end at last, I say to myself. I hear a low murmur of conversation behind that door. I hang my overcoat on a rail in the corridor before I let myself in to the Events Room. In this hall, effect a small groups of middle-aged or elderly men, separated out from each other in a sort of human archipelago, converse quietly with each other. The occasion is almost exclusively masculine. Suits and ties appear to be *de rigueur*. The participants in each of these conversational islands are all fully acquainted with each other, obviously. They display no desire to integrate new members into their groups. Glasses of red wine are clasped in fists. Waiters move from group to group, offering cocktail sausages on wooden toothpicks from ceramic bowls.

As I appear in the doorway, inquisitive eyes scrutinize me from head to toe. Before their owners withdraw their gaze, returning to whatever arcane discussions they are having with members of their conversational circle. The occasional face here and there resuscitates faint, and unwelcome, memories of times long past. The ubiquitous Dr. Beggan, "the man who put reconciliation on a firm commercial basis", being a case in hand. However, that particular worthy affects not to recognize me. And I prefer it like that...

A rapid scan of those present in the hall lets me know that the Cardinal has yet to arrive.

Copies of Quinn's *Gaelic Presbyterians of Fermanagh* are

stacked up on the table just inside the doorway. There is a colored picture of a lakeside—Lough Erne being the lake in question, doubtlessly—on the cover of this publication which is to be launched here tonight by Cardinal Ó Fiaich. I pick up one copy—which turns out to be a mere booklet of 32 pages, a bespectacled young lady sitting behind the table scrutinizing me suspiciously as I do so.

That will cost you 5 pounds sterling, she says.

All I want is a review copy of the booklet for *The Belfast Courier*, say I, as I flash my press card.

Oh I'm so sorry, sir, but I will have to discuss that with the organizer of this event.

She is referring, doubtlessly, to Beggan, chairperson of Reconciliation Limited, who is now standing close to the door, a glass of mineral water in his hand. He has selected this strategic vantage point—unless I am sadly mistaken in regard to my memories of Beggan—so that he will be the first to greet his old pal, the Cardinal, when the latter emerges through the doorway to join the company.

Not that Beggan gives a tinker's curse about religion, its works and pomps. *No sirree!* Absolutely not! It is an indelible part of Reconciliation folklore that Beggan once remarked: "we have traveled far beyond God", in response to the unfortunate remark of an assistant of his who said "thanks be to God", on hearing that a dubious Reconciliation check had failed to bounce.

However, the social standing and political connections of an individual always takes priority over whatever distaste Beggan may have for her or his religious or ideological baggage.

Let that bastard take two copies if that is what he wants, I overhear Beggan say to the girl.

The grin under that famous Hitlerian moustache reminds me

of a shark's mouth as he comes over to join me.

So, Mike, I understand that you're working now for the *Northern Courier*, he says. Well, I hope that your crowd does not fall under the influence of Moscow, or worse: the damned propaganda mill of West Belfast. Not like other editors we could name and who we have had the misfortune of knowing in recent years.

I refuse to rise to the bait.

The imagined slyness of his humor causes him to emit a chuckle. I detect the old familiar heavy smell of gin and vermouth on his breath. Certain things never change.

It's too bad the Presbyterians are afraid to come here tonight, says Beggan. Thanks to last night's horror show perpetrated by that murder gang, and not under the influence of certain anonymous inflammatory material in your newspaper, I hope, reconciliation has been put back years... You'll find wine and sandwiches on the table over there...Talk to me later...And he turns brusquely away from me. Giving me to understand, unequivocally, that our conversation is over.

Since nobody joins me, I make for a table groaning under its display of bottles of wine, along with trays heaped with sandwiches and salt crackers adorned with anchovies, pate, olives and slices of assorted cheeses. A waiter fills a glass with red wine and hands it to me. I turn around to examine the crowd assembled here more closely—which is swelling according as new suits arrive on the scene—when a voice beside me greeted me in Irish.

Well, Mike, long time no see! How are you keeping these days?

Nigel Hamilton, a photographer from the enemy camp, *The Northern Messenger*, greets me thus. Bursting with his customary good humor! A large leather camera case is slung over his right shoulder.

Not a complaint in the world, I say. The usual lie! But tell me this, Nigel, where did you ever pick up those words of Irish?

These are the only words of bog Irish I have, says Hamilton, as he retreats to the comfort zone of Shankill English, his native idiom. They tell me that that is the way to greet the jailbird comrades of your Long Kesh mob, he says. But tell me this! Are you here out of interest? Or are you here to cover the event for the *Courier*?

To cover the event, just like you, I'm afraid!

Yep! Well, I'm here to get a shot of the Cardinal talking to some of the more exalted members of my own supposed religion. If they dare show up after last night, that is. But I hope to hell that your guy, Ó Fiaich—an old pal of old Gusty Spence, if this story that your crowd ran with a few weeks ago is true—doesn't keep us waiting too long. The game will be starting in 40 minutes time, he says—looking hurriedly at his watch—and I promised the moon and the stars to the lads that I would join them for a few drinks to watch and enjoy the slaughter.

So your money will be on Hearts, you unrepentant Orange bastard, I say mockingly.

Our comradely banter, born of a common journalistic calling, makes light of sectarian divisions. There you have it, you dyed in the wool Fenian mother-fucker!

A hand now taps my left shoulder. I still recognize the sound of the voice that now addresses itself to me, although it is percolated through the filter of many years. It is none other than that of Richard—Dick—Goggin, chief executive of Reconciliation Limited. I turn to face him, noting again that faint courteous smile, a deceptive mask that is his stock in trade.

I remind myself to watch carefully what I say. For Dick is a tricky customer. It is said that if Donald is the bad cop of

Reconciliation, Dick very willingly plays the role of good cop. But that tricky twosome are forever in cahoots with each other, according to stories widely broadcast by Reconciliation's many enemies. The same enemies are largely made up of disaffected ex-employees of Reconciliation.

Through frequently expressing his sympathies with the organization's staff and his pretended disagreement with policies being promoted by Beggan, Dick succeeds in ingratiating himself with Reconciliation's foot soldiers. Thence, he is the first to recognize signs of staff disaffection. And of course, he is the mole who keeps Donald fully informed as to what is stirring in the lower echelons of Reconciliation.

As I turn to face Dick, the latter stretches out his right hand. And, having no good reason now to be still in an adversarial mood, I grasp and shake it.

Forgive me if I seem to be butting in on your conversation says Dick courteously to Hamilton. But I haven't seen this man, referring to me, for ages... You are Mike O'Rourke, of course, he says, looking me up and down. Unless I be greatly mistaken! Donald has just told me that you had just arrived. I am very happy to see you again and you are most welcome here. I always enjoy your articles in the *Northern Courier.* I must say that Donald detects a whiff of left wing ideology from your present work. Your knee-jerk support for strikers, for example. And he thinks that your constant harping on the issue of civil rights for Catholics lends aid and comfort to the terrorists. However, I don't think that the clash of different points of view is at all bad, *per se.* On the contrary! Constant exposure to other points of view is what oils and fertilizes the democratic process. Just as long as the writer doesn't go overboard with some crazy bias or other! Be all that as it may, you are here to cover the event, Donald has just told me.

We are talking, man to man, by his time, separated out from the general throng who are now clustered like barnacles along the wine bar. Dick lowers his voice to a whisper, just as if he were about to divulge a secret: We are quite concerned. The Cardinal should have arrived long before this. And Donald is worried that he has not yet arrived. And, as luck would have it, we have no copy of his speech to hand. After that hideous slaughter in the Rangers bar last night, one wouldn't know what to make of this delay. Most of the Presbyterians who were invited have indicated to us that they will not be coming. Their nervousness is understandable. Especially when you take into account the revenge threat of the UDA...

However, we give his Lordship another half hour. And if he had not arrived by that time, well, we will just have to proceed with the launch without him. Donald has spoken to Colm O'Donnell, and he says that he is willing to stand in for the Cardinal, if it comes to that... But now let me introduce you now to the author of the *Gaelic Presbyterians of Fermanagh* himself.

And Goggin led me across to the corner of the hall from which Dr. Hugh Quinn, ME, PhD, a tall untidy gray-haired man, was casting his pearls. A luminary of Opus Dei, if they can work to be believed, according to Beggan, who harbors the same animosity towards Quinn as he does, apparently, towards the bulk of the human race.

There is a man here from the *Northern Courier* who would like to speak to you, says Goggin.

That, of course, is an outstandingly factual inaccuracy. The man from the *Northern Courier* has not the slightest desire to engage with the learned Dr. Quinn. All I had hoped to this evening is integrate an extract from Ó Fiaich's speech into a report whose broad general lines are already written in my head: Protestants and the Irish Language... Archbishop Bedell's Bible... William Neilson... Charlotte Brooke... Our common Gaelic heritage...*lilibulero, lilibulero bullenalaa*[3]... the Gaelic Presbyterians of the Hebrides...

---

[3] *A popular Ulster Unionist ballad. The words from Irish Gaelic translate as:*

Not forgetting to add a couple of sentences regarding Fermanagh's Gaelic Presbyterians, stolen from Quinn's Introduction to his work, to bring the report fully up to date. That should be more than enough to satisfy McCafferty for whom, like the vast majority of his countrymen, the Irish language and its affairs are *terra incognita*...

But, of course, good manners require that I say something to Quinn. Something obvious like:

Whatever possessed you to take an interest in Fermanagh's Irish speakers?

Well, my grandmother, may God be merciful to her, got to know an old Protestant woman of Scottish descent, originally from Manor Hamilton, who spoke the most fluent Irish. And this is what she always spoke, Irish, her normal day to day language, as her own people knew little English...

But isn't Manor Hamilton in County Leitrim? I interject innocently. And your book has to do, I believe, with the Irish spoken in Fermanagh.

Of course! I explain all of that in the book. The Great Hunger caused herself and her family to move to Aldermody, near Enniskillen, when she herself was only a girl. The really interesting thing was that the classical dative plural case of the older language was preserved in the everyday speech of these poor Presbyterians. I deal with all of that in my book.

With all respect, I don't agree with any of that, said a small bespectacled man, who had been listening in on our conversation, somewhat fiercely. My name is Brendan Abbot. And I would like to say that, whatever about your Fermanagh Protestants, Irish is now a Catholic language. And always will be, please God. No matter what grammatical cases were, if they were indeed, in the mouths of some Fermanagh Prods centuries ago. Take our old Irish blessings, for

---

*"the lily was triumphant, we won the day"*.

example! Could you imagine our native Irish blessings, suffused as they are by our Catholic heritage, our love of Mary, the mother of God, in the mouths of the Linfield mob? If you uttered but a single word of Irish in Drumcree, your life would be at risk.

I hope I am not butting in here, says another voice, speaking half in Irish, half in English, but I don't agree with anything you are saying.

I recognize the speaker immediately, although I haven't heard his voice for more than twenty years. It is that of the macaronic[4] madman, Michael J. Maley, unless I be very much mistaken.

Not only is it a part of what we are, it's a part of what we all are. And I emphasize the word all. For Irish belongs to Prods, Cats, Jews, Commies, Orangies, Mahomedans; you name it. The whole shaggin' shebang, as the ould poet once said...

And then, buttonholing me, so to speak:

It's great to see you again after all those years, Mike. But your glass is empty. Give it to me and I'll get you a refill.

I marvel at how the lingo the macaronic madman speaks has degenerated over the last twenty years. It is such a linguistic patchwork, whose essential meaning is so often carried by English words and phrases, that it can hardly be categorized any longer as Irish. Or as English! As he weaves his way back towards me, I am saved from the tedium of his company by two handclaps into a microphone from Goggin, who is now standing on a small stage facing us.

The crowd responds by reducing its conversational buzz to a hushed silence. As soon the conversational level reaches, for him, an acceptable minimum, Goggin proceeds with his valiant effort to rescue the night's proceedings:

---

[4]  *One who speaks a mixture of two or more languages.*

I am afraid that the Cardinal will not be able to be with us tonight. *(Predictable groans of disappointment).* I was talking to his Eminence on the phone a few minutes ago and he told me that he had left Armagh in good time so as to be with us here for this important event. However, such was the extent of traffic build-ups due to the prevalence of army and police check-points on all main roads that he realized that there was no way he could make it here on time. So, regretfully, he was obliged to return to Armagh. He asked me to convey his regrets to all of you here and, most especially, to Dr. Hugh Quinn, whom he congratulates on his achievement, and to wish us every success with this launch of *Presbyterian Irish Speakers* of Fermanagh. A prolonged handclap follows this statement.

Therefore, as long as we are all assembled here, continues Goggin, I will ask Colm O'Donnell—author, journalist, radio and television broadcaster, who is known to, and well-respected by, all of us—to launch Hugh Quinn's magnificent booklet, *Presbyterian Irish Speakers of Fermanagh.* And to terminate the first part of the proceedings, what I will call "The Speech Aspect" of this occasion, the Reverend Ian Nicholson, a Presbyterian friend, tells me that he would like to share some recollections he has of the Irish speakers in his own parish when he was new to his ministry. But, in the meantime, I would ask Colm to come up here and give *Presbyterian Irish Speakers of Fermanagh* the baptism it so richly deserves. *(Loud applause!)*

At this juncture, I was in two minds. Would this Reverend Nicholson, the only Presbyterian at this *soiree,* it seems, have anything to say that might be of any news value? I already knew, of course, that O'Donnell was a past master in the art of hot air production and that his speech would present a medley of fact, half-fact and self-aggrandizing fiction to vie for the listener's attention. So much blah-blah, arguably! But a well-performed blah-blah, artistically speaking, as his references to his contacts with his many friends in high places, especially if they are deceased, are always bound to be highly entertaining.

My watch informs me that it is 6.33 p.m. If I made my exit now, I would still have time to see most of that game in Parkhead. However, and the author of the book that is about to be launched standing beside me, it would be churlish of me to leave right now. As I stood there, between two minds, so to speak, I felt a light tap on my left shoulder. I turned around. Nigel Hamilton was standing there.

I wonder could you do me a big favor, Mike, he says. I have to call the office to let them know that your guru, the Cardinal, will not be arriving. Nor those Presbyterians who were supposed to have come here either! To tell you the truth, I don't think that a Prod photographer like me has any business at all being here if hardly any of my crowd show up. So, could you keep an eye on my camera over there on that chair while I make my call? It's an expensive German make so don't let any budding demon press photographer make off with it. I shouldn't be too long.

No problem, I say. I'll put it here on this chair beside me to guard it with my life until you come back. Away with you now and make your phone call!

The names of Gaeldom's Protestant pantheon are being invoked by O'Donnell as I turn my attention back to the stage. Bedell... Neilson... Vallancey... Adams... Brooke... But for the brilliant pioneering work of these Protestant Gaels, the Irish language would not be heard in this hall tonight. I see Abbott's head shaking directly in front of me, giving to understand that at least one person here disagrees with O'Donnell's reading of the history of the Irish language.

Further on into the speech, other names emerged from the same stock to fight the good linguistic fight: Douglas Hyde, Ernest Blythe and Risteárd Ó Glaisne, to cull but a few names from O'Donnell's lengthy litany of Protestant language activists.

Therefore, it is right and proper, he says, that the Protestant Gaels of Ireland be commemorated here tonight. And we are heavily indebted to Dr. Hugh Quinn, who is with us here, for the extra light he has thrown on this important, on this essential, part of our common heritage. *(Loud applause)*.

I knew, and knew very well, Hugh's father, Lawrence—or Larry—Quinn. He was forever a Gael and a republican to the very marrow of his bones *(Applause)*. And even if he never mastered the intricacies of the Irish language—and those of you who live here in the Six County state understand the official attitudes that have left Irish marginalized here—Larry made certain that his family, Jacinta, Lourdes, Pacella, Benedict and Eugene here, came into contact with the very best of spoken Irish, in the heart of the Rannafast Gaeltacht *(Applause)*. A Gael to the very marrow of his bones was Larry, as I have said. In his love for our native music and games he yielded to nobody. And I am certain, doubly certain, that we can say the same of Hugh, a true son of his father, whose book I have the honor to launch here tonight. A book which we will doubtlessly find to be redolent of the noblest aspirations of the Gaelic spirit.

And now I have a confession to make. I have to admit that I still have to read this extraordinary book. To tell you the honest truth, I didn't get to see it until a few moments ago. I only arrived back from South Africa last night after interviewing an old friend of mine there. I am sure that all of you here have heard of my interviewee. Nelson Mandela. And do you know what Nelson told me as we had a drink together in Soweto after our work? Colm, he said, you in Ireland have a basic lesson to learn from the tragic history of South Africa. Never forget the understanding we gained from the long years of strife in our country! And it is this: the deeper the wound the greater is the need for the poultice of reconciliation. I will repeat again what my friend Nelson told me: the deeper the wound, the greater is the need for the poultice of reconciliation.

Let us meditate on those noble words that I heard two days

ago from the mouth of a friend of mine and one of the people who has suffered most in our epoch in the cause of human dignity and freedom. And remember them again especially when you are buying this marvelous little book that Hugh Quinn has made available to us. Remember that this book is another important step in the direction of reconciliation and mutual understanding that is so badly needed in these cruel days. As was tragically demonstrated last night in the Rangers bar in this very city.

Therefore, let me say again that it is a great honor for me—and I am sorry that my good friend, Tomás Ó Fiaich, is not here to perform this most pleasant task—it gives me the greatest of pleasure to announce that a crucially important contribution to the reconciliation process, the *Gaelic Presbyterians of Fermanagh*, by Doctor Hugh Quinn, is now officially launched...

I find it difficult to contain my laughter. A vintage performance! O'Donnell is a word wizard without any shadow of doubt. From absolutely nothing, from this extraordinary book that the rogue had never read, from an imagined interview with one of the major personality of our times, from his acquaintanceship with Larry Quinn—if such ever existed—O'Donnell had concocted a marvelously constructed speech to take the place of that of the Cardinal, confined to his palace in Armagh by military activity on the roads.

As Goggin reclaims the microphone, Hugh Quinn, beside me, is taking a nervous last-minute look at notes he had prepared to respond to the golden-tongued O'Donnell. Judging by the thickness of his sheaf of papers it is clear that Quinn plans to regale us with more than the customary few words. I plan to make my escape. With the applause for O'Donnell still in my ears, I glance again at my watch. It is two minutes past 7 p.m.. I could still see the second half of the game if I uprooted myself now from this occasion.

However I can hardly take my leave just yet since Nigel Hamilton has yet to return to reclaim the camera that I had committed myself to guard for him. Trapped!

Quinn was on his way to the stage when the lights went out. Suddenly the hotel's Event Room was plunged into pitch-black darkness. From the frenzied hubbub of voices around me, I heard someone proclaim that the door of the hall was locked. Another voice claimed that the premises could be exited through an emergency door at its rear. But since there is no light, I am unable to orientate myself to move towards the rear of the hall. I have never imagined darkness as thick as this. The clamor around me abates little by little. And as silence now appears to be installing itself in my surrounds, I began to panic and imagine that I have been abandoned here in this pitch darkness.

Is there anybody else here apart from myself, I call out. I can't see a damn thing in this darkness...

Another voice answers me. And I immediately recognize that Hugh Quinn, the author, is cooped up in here with me.

I am rooting around among these chairs trying to find my briefcase, he says. But, like you, I cannot see a damn thing here. I haven't a clue where the rest of the people have gone. But I do have a small torch in my bag if only I could lay my hands on it. Do you think that we are the only ones left in this hall?

Michael J. Maley here, says a voice, rather close by. I think that we are the only ones left here, as you say. Hello there!  Can anybody else hear us?

I can hear you, says another voice. Here I am, as large as life!

Great, says Quinn. But who are you?

Me?  I am Brendan Abbott. John Joe to you! There must be some sort of power cut. But what I would like to find out is how the others managed to get out.

They found the emergency exit, it seems, I say. Now, if only somebody here only had a couple of matches! Or that torch you mentioned, Hugh!

I think I have found that accursed bag at last, Quinn's disembodied voice booms out of the darkness. Patience is the cardinal virtue in these circumstances, my friends. Hold on a minute or two! Ah, I can feel that torch now with my fingers. There, I have it at last!

A few seconds later, the weak light of Quinn's torch shows me that the other three men, Quinn, Maley and Abbott, together with myself are now the sole inhabitants of the hall. There is no sign of Hamilton's camera anywhere. Its owner must have showed up before the lights went out and managed to retrieve it just before the power failure. He might, at least, have thanked me for looking after his property! I then notice that the talk on the wall is frozen at two minutes past 7 p.m. Of course, stupid! That was the time the electricity must have been cut...

Let us head quickly for the emergency door, says Maley. This goddam place is too damn spooky for me. It gives me the heebie-jeebies. What time is it, by the way?

It is exactly 2 minutes after seven, says Quinn, squinting at his watch.

Your watch must have stopped, says Maley. It was that time a while ago. But, God help us, it seems that you are correct. That is what my watch tells me also... Look! Here is the emergency door.

It's shut, say I. Let us hope that it is not locked!

When we manage, finally, to open the door, the solidity of the darkness outside takes all of us aback. The weak light of our torch is unable to penetrate it. Nor can we see the stars above through it. It is an opaque darkness that appears to be composed of a thick viscous material that is completely impermeable to light.

Now, what the hell are we going to do? I hear Quinn say behind me.

Get pissed! Opportunity knocks but once! says Maley. The bar attendants appear to have fucked off somewhere. But all of their bottles are still on the table.

Whatever the hell we are going to do, we had better do it quickly, says Quinn, paying no attention whatsoever to Maley's recommendation. The battery in this torch is not going to last forever.

I don't know about you lot, but I have no intention of hanging around here for much longer, says Abbott. I have to be in Limavady by midday tomorrow to sign an important contract.

But the dark outside is almost like glue, says Maley from the open emergency door. I stuck my foot into it and when I tried to pull it out it was like trying to pull my foot from out of a swamp.

This is a time for lateral thinking, says Quinn briskly. I saw a long coiled rope at the back of the hall earlier on. Suppose Mike here and I tie ourselves to this rope, and try to head out into the dark, then we will quickly see if we can make any headway through it... Since we will both be connected by the rope we will not lose contact with each other... John Joe here can hold on to the end of the rope. In this way, if the pair of us go astray outside, we will always able to return here by just following the rope.

A great idea, Quinn! But we had better try this idea out immediately. Because, since we left the emergency door open some of that dark outside seems to be seeping into the hall here.

Give us a song, somebody, says Maley. Has anybody got an oul' song there? If you do sing a song, sing an Irish song, as the poet said in those good oul' days that are gone forever. A long time ago there was this man who lived on the top of a mountain. And a long time ago it was. Come on, man, just one oul' song!

Quinn and I quickly locate the rope and tie ourselves to it. Thus linked, we head out from the emergency door, for all the world like a some mountaineering twosome hell-bent on reaching the summit of Everest. If such were necessary to release us from our incarceration in the hotel's event room, then so be it! However, a couple of steps suffice to show us clearly that escape by this method is impossible. Apart from being unable to see the ground beneath our feet, the greatest obstacle to our progress is the sheer solid consistency of the darkness itself. Because of its putty-like resistance, Quinn and I are unable neither to see each other nor advance more than a few steps. Indeed, I am unable to see my own hand when I hold it up close to my face, right in front of my eyes.

Not only that, but every step taken through that medium freezes us to the very marrow of our bones, and the first half dozen steps outside takes us half an hour, at least, and leaves us totally exhausted. We have no recourse but to abandon our efforts and return to base.

After our return to the safety of the hall, Maley announces joyously that he had liberated another bottle of whiskey that he had discovered by groping around in the dark under the counter.

Abbott returns to a favorite theme of his. Fermanagh Protestants could never have spoken Irish, in spite of Quinn's assertion to the contrary. Not to mention the retention of the dative case of classical Irish in their everyday speech! Pure balderdash! Everybody knows that Protestants would rather commit mass hara-kiri than speak a Catholic lingo, no matter what Quinn has to say about the matter.

What about Douglas Hyde,then? asks Quinn, satisfied that he has punctured the sectarian bias of Abbott with one simple question. He fails to see, however, the ace that is lurking up Abbott's sleeve.

Ah, but he has to do with the Free State, says Abbott triumphantly. I am talking about our local Prods. About th'oul Orangies...

> In the County Tyrone,
> in the town of Dungannon,
> 'Twas many a ruction myself had a hand in,
> There dwelt there Bob Williamson,
> a weaver by trade,
> And all of us thought him a stout Orange blade...

sings Maley hoarsely and raucously, whatever shyness that may have been inhibiting his musical talents blown now to the four winds by the whisky. Come on, lads, he says, stop taking our predicament so seriously. We have all the time in the world now to make hay while the sun shines.

There is damn all sun shining in this goddam place, says Quinn dryly.

You are dead right there, says Maley. What there is of sun here in this kip—every golden drop of it—is shining here out of this bottle.

The four of us sit around, bottles being passed from mouth to mouth. Arguing. Retelling old tales. Dozing. Wondering how long it is going to take our rescuers to reach us. In the dark most of the time in order to conserve the torch battery.

The hours pass as slow as each eternity itself, as is always the case in contexts of total uncertainty. We have no idea what time it is even. One of us goes to the emergency door every so often to see if the first light of dawn is visible. But no faint blush of light, leavening the darkness without, gives us any grounds for hope that a new day is hurrying towards us. Indeed, all of our watches indicate that time itself has stopped, frozen in its tracks. At two minutes past 7 p.m., to be brutally accurate.

I am sleeping deeply, Jennifer in her white silk nightgown approaching me in the bedroom of my dream, when Quinn's voice in my ear awakens me from that pleasant stupor. The hall is still in pitch darkness.

Do you know what the time is, I ask mechanically, still in that halfway house between sleep and wakefulness.

Quinn emitted a small rueful laugh before he answered me.

What do you think yourself, Mike? Two minutes after 7 p.m., of course; how the hell would I know, no more than yourself, what the correct time is? But look here!

He turned on his torch and directed its week beam of light on to a small radio he was holding in his hand.

I had forgotten that I was carrying this gadget in a pocket of my jacket. Why don't we turn it on to see if we can find any information about this god-awful plight we find ourselves in!

In the weak light of the torch I see him press a button and the radio comes to life. It is a relief to know that the outside world still exists and that we should have some contact with it, however tenuous, with its works and pomps.

The comforting sound of the Gaeltacht Radio's Jew's harp signature tune puts us, at least imaginatively, in contact with day-to-day normality.

It must be daylight already if that sound is coming over the airwaves, opines Abbott, who is awakened now by the merry clanging of the station's signature Jew's harp.

Maley is softly snoring somewhere outside the range of the torch-light.

But if, indeed, morning has arrived, how come this darkness hangs on in here and outside the door? And to where did all of the other guests who were attending the event disappear? Will the radio be able to explain to us the persistence of this night darkness after the dawn? We know full well that the news will follow directly the station's signature tune. And, as the twanging of the Jew's harp ceases, here comes the voice from outside we have been waiting for: *This is Gaeltacht Radio*, says the announcer. *It is now eight o'clock in the morning. And here now are the headlines of the national and international news being read to you by Seosamh Ó Cuaig.*

We here will hang on to the newsreader's every word, eager to pick up some vital clue from a voice that appears to us listeners in the dark to emanate from some imagined world on some far distant galaxy. Words that will, hopefully, penetrate the darkness outside and inside and cast some light on our plight:

*It is now believed that loyalist paramilitaries caused the huge explosion last night in the Ulster Arms Hotel, Belfast, that killed four persons at least, and left 23 wounded, some seriously. All of them were attending be launching of an Irish-language book,* Gaelic Presbyterians of Fermanagh, *in the hall of the hotel at the time of the explosion. This act has been condemned strongly by both the Taoiseach[5] and the British Prime Minister, who promised that the security forces would not let up their search for both the perpetrators*

---

[5] *Irish prime minister*

*of this barbarous outrage, as he called it, and that of the previous night at the Rangers bar, Belfast, in order that they be brought as speedily as possible to justice.*

*Cardinal Tomas Ó Fiaich, was to have launched the book at the Ulster Arms Hotel, and the security authorities believe he may have been the intended target of loyalist terrorists seeking revenge for the Rangers Bar attack that has now left eight dead. But, because of the frequency of checkpoints being operated on the road between Armagh and Belfast by the RUC and the British Army, the Cardinal was unable to reach the hotel in time for the book launch. He returned, accordingly, to Armagh. The police have the names of those killed in the attack, according to an RUC spokesperson. But their names will be withheld until all of their close relatives have been informed.*

*Speaking from Armagh, Cardinal Ó Fiaich said that...*

We look around at each other.

Dumbfounded!

Just as both torch and radio batteries give out...

# A WARNING TO OUR NEIGHBORS

**DEAREST NEIGHBORS:**

We wish to take this opportunity to warn you and your neighbors to be increasingly vigilant in the coming days, weeks, months and, probably, for the foreseeable future. Let us explain to you the context in which we issue such an unexpected and, perhaps for some delicate souls, rather alarming warning!

We mental health professionals are working in the new psychiatric institute recently established in your neighborhood. Or, to be perfectly clear, we work in your local "prison" or "penitentiary", if you are addicted to such antiquated terminology. (Indeed, the very use of the terms "prisoner", "convict" and "sociopath" is banned within the confines of our Institute, and even that seemingly innocuous word, "patient" is taboo here). "Guest" is our only recommended designation for such persons, no matter what unfortunate, (we never use the word "criminal") lifestyle decisions have led them to take advantage of the various "cutting edge" therapies we have on offer here.

Occasionally, one hears the view expressed—in secretive whispers, of course—that the older non-politically correct designations were more *ad rem*, that is, more efficient at turning our guests into the normalized submissive and productive citizens that our society, continually and insistently, craves. But, having little interest in discussing such recidivist ideas, we have no intention of exposing you to the cut and thrust of that superannuated controversy here.

Our work here can be very intellectually and emotionally stimulating. Consider the range of characters we have here among us on our campus, and you will see immediately what we mean. There are, almost literally, hundreds of them: Jesus Christ, Marilyn Monroe (all of whom are not necessarily of the female gender), Brian Boru, Osama bin Laden, Leopold Bloom, Saint Patrick, La Belle Dame sans Merci, Marlon Brando (all of whom are not necessarily males), Don Quixote, Franz Kafka, Wolfe Tone, Madonna, Caitríona Pháidín[6], Hamlet, Catherine the Great of Russia... each one of which has his, or her, unique story to tell. And what you have here is but a limited selection of the "masks" (as we call them here ) that are chosen—and worn—by the guests of this Institute of ours.

If the clues we have given you up to now are insufficient for you to get the drift of my meaning, let me try to explain the jist of the innovative therapy that is being tested here in a terminology that will be, mercifully for you, free from technical jargon.

In the first place, we deal here with souls that are wounded, defective or otherwise deficient, in ways that have been found to be non-amenable to conventional therapies. As the worries and insecurities that accompany our present dispensation make the yoke of normality increasingly difficult to bear, the incidence of such maimed souls is steadily on the increase.

The therapy employed here is based on the proven success of similar programs in Milwaukee and in Santa Barbara in the United

---

[6] *The principal character of the most innovative 20th century Irish Gaelic novel,* Cré na Cille (Graveyard Clay) *by Máirtín Ó'Cadhain.*

States. The basic principle is that lived fantasy lives that counteract the psychological wear and tear of modern stress can serve as nuclei, as it were, about which new and successfully functioning personalities—in acceptable contemporary terms—can be made to crystallize.

Consider the prevalence of such spontaneous fantasy self-imaging in the world about us. The fragmented personalities of our modern era reconstituting themselves as integrated personalities that are felt to be strong and successful, say, by the subject in question! Troubled teenagers, for example, whose behaviors and accents mimic those of some famous footballer or other, are a case in hand, or others who model their gear and gestures on those of pop-stars and other much-publicized media personalities, as detailed by their respective publicity agents!

You will, doubtlessly, have heard of lumpenprole sociopaths becoming Adolf Hitler, imaginatively speaking! Or intense members of the infantile left, as Lenin described revolutionaries who believe in the magical power of simplistic formulae to overthrow the current order, and who often model their polemics and behavior along the style of an imagined Vladimir Ilych or an imagined Big Mao of the Little Red Book.

Here in this Institute, however, such personality reconstruction is undertaken comprehensively and scientifically. Through systematic analysis of the broken personalities of our guests, the fantasies—we call them masks—best adapted to an optimal reintegration of the personality are identified. Once the target personality has been identified, and subject to the guest's agreement, we provide the resources—psychological counseling, clothes, hypnotherapy, literature, DVDs, videos etc.—appropriate to a successful appropriation of the mask in question. And, above all, we provide a safe sanctuary for the guests as they habituate themselves to their new assumed personalities. Until the wearing of their new masks becomes as automatic and as natural to them as flight is to birds or swimming is to fish...

The new masks that are assembled and fitted here provide solid psychological bases for emotional lives that had previously been disordered, even chaotic. In this way, the staff of our Institute—all expert technologists of fantasy—create psychological order, stability and organization where emotional and intellectual anarchy reigned previously, along with doubt, enervating uncertainty and total failure to establish realistic and socially acceptable goals.

To be totally honest, dear neighbor, the world will become a much better place thanks to the expertise of the staff of our Institute...

So, "The Mask Boutique" is the name they give to this particular corner (there are others) of our Institute. However, there are many other boutiques on the wide expanse of our campus. If we fail to locate an appropriate mask for a particular guest here, then he or she could well be directed to the Pharmaceutical Boutique, which offers a range of poultices for the soul: Prozac, Xanax, Paxil, Effexor, Seropram *et cetera.* However, such a resort is still largely theoretical as far as we are concerned. For, it is the proud boast of the staff of our Mask Boutique that they have yet to admit defeat and send one of their clients into the clutches of the Pharmaceutical Boutique operatives.

However, this clean record, of which we are justifiably proud, is being placed in some considerable jeopardy by our latest guest, Mr. Psycho, his designated pseudonym until we manage to locate an appropriate mask for him. This gentleman has been with us for some months now, with no progress whatsoever to show for our efforts with him over that period. Apart from that, the report he prepared for us gives us—and you also, dear neighbor—more than ample cause for serious concern as long as he remains here in our neighborhood.

We have read this report many times. However, it has failed so far to give us any workable clue as to what mask, out of the wide selection history and modern life makes available, would be adequate to the reformation of Psycho's character. Indeed it has sometimes occurred to us that he is so deeply disturbed that there is no place left in his heart—if that were indeed the *mot juste*—for self-doubt or for fantasy.

The aspect of this particular guest, however, would never give you to understand that he was suffering from any known malady. Because, unbelievably, he is the quietest and most mannerly guest we have ever had on our campus. He appears every day at spick and span as a tailor's dummy. His close-shaven cheeks as smooth as a baby's backside! The shine from his boots rivals sunlight! Displaying the suave and elegant manners of a previous generation! A never-failing courteous smile forever on his lips! The one person in this experimental Institute who is 100% normal, you would say, unless you were made aware of the full facts of his case.

But the external characteristics of Mr. Psycho should never fool anybody. Read for yourself, dear neighbor extracts from his own account of the events that led to his being our guest. For your own comfort, I have censored those elements of his text that have most disturbed members of our own Institute staff who, believe me, have seen almost everything:

*At the time in question, I was preparing for the visit of my boss and his wife to our house. It was not at my behest that this visit was about to take place. Quite the contrary! But Helen, my wife, has been incessantly nagging me over the last number of weeks to invite them to visit us. And, at last, I acceded to her wish, though with ill-grace. The things one will do, the hoops one will jump through, to earn a quiet life!*

*I myself see no reason for this visitation. What would I have to say to this Brendan J. Blake, to name the boss more fully! And still less to his Gorgon wife, the unbearable Eilish? My misgivings about this* visit I explained, more times than I care to mention, to Helen. For all the good that did me! No matter what I said, that halfwit felt that it would be "nice" to extend an invitation to that loathsome twosome to pay a visit to our modest abode. And, who knows, maybe such a social call will help you to ascend the company ladder a little more rapidly, she said. If only she knew the levels of self-debasement that such ascents demand!

How I hated Blake, who understood perfectly the greater effectiveness of the carrot than the whip as an instrument for extracting the pound of flesh from the bones of his employees.

Were there elements of jealousy woven through this hatred, as Helen was so readily disposed to allege? Who knows! The ultimate roots of human motivation are still a mystery in spite of the unending guff of the shrinks and the fools who believe them. In any case, this bloodsucker swam into my ken each day, a crease in his trousers on which one could pare pencils, his hair slicked back with some aromatic oil or other. His cynical courtesy, his never-failing good humor, the ready smile—and I was not the only one to detect its lupine subtext!— perpetually hovering about the corners of his mouth.

It was thanks to the coming visit of this bandit and his garrulous consort that I had to act the clown that evening. So, there I was, wearing a multicolored apron, and putting the final touches to the hors d'ouvres that will be scoffed a little later on by these unwelcome (by me) guests, as we wait for the doorbell to ring. Any minute now!

So it came to be, alas! Helen came tripping down the stairs, breathless, to welcome the new arrivals. From the kitchen I could hear them in the hallway, the womenfolk—Helen and the unbearable Eilish—chirruping at each other like excited birds.

We haven't seen each other for ages, my dear, etc. et cetera. Into the sitting room with them. We have such a busy social life these days, I hear the Blake Gorgon bleat, that we have hardly any time for *our old acquaintances. We are only just recovering from the Minister's party last night. It was amazing; everybody who was anybody was there. The Taoiseach himself showed up for a short while...*

*Oh, you have done up the place beautifully, Helen, since we were here last. You have done a fantastic job. And I note that you have changed the curtains also, unless I am much mistaken. They remind me of the old curtains we used to have before we changed them last spring. What do you think, Brendan?*

*Brendan Blake, Esq. says that, indeed, they reminded him of the old curtains in his own house. And that he had left those with Oxfam some months ago. His quiet authoritative voice emphasized his wife's judgment. My God, when I think of that poisonous Gorgon! And those bloody curtains! I hoped that the scatterbrain, Helen, would have at least the common sense to not divulge the household secret: namely, that we ourselves had acquired those new curtains from Oxfam some months ago. She had that much sense that night, though that particular commodity was not her forté...*

*Helen had already filled the sherry glasses by the time that I joined the others in the sitting room. Carrying a tray on which were plates containing smoked salmon, pâté de foie gras and a selection of cheeses, all on salt crackers. Brendan loves pâté, said Helen, from wherever she elicited that fact.*

*Great to see you outside their salt mine, old pal, said Blake, giving me that stereotypic masculine greeting of a buddy-buddy puck in the biceps. His assumed bonhomie did not extend to mentioning my name, however, whether by ignorance, design or, a most unlikely, though welcome, possibility, an early onset of Alzheimer's. I see that Helen is keeping you well harnessed, he says. That eternally present bland malice lurked behind his smile revealing itself momentarily, as he glanced amusedly at the apron I had forgotten to remove before joining that meaningless huddle in the sitting room .*

*This bastard, Blake, belonged to a new breed, to a new*

*mutation of the species that is rapidly changing for the worse the dynamic of our human ecosystem, I remember saying to myself. Like weeds taking over an abandoned graveyard. Ignorant freebooters who question nothing and whose sole concern is to fatten their own bank accounts and whose arrogant certainties are never challenged by the embarrassment of self-doubt! Greed is good, they chant in staccato chorus, as onwards they march, secure in their ruthless self-confidence. They place the universal measuring stick of profitability beside good and evil, justice and injustice, good and bad citizenship. The cancerous growth of their bank accounts is unceasing. Their insolent opinions fester in the body politic...*

*Helen is star-struck by the arrant nonsense—sound common sense, he himself would say—of the opinions being mouthed by Blake.*

*Ireland is an amazing country, he says. It could be the best small country in the world! If only we could get an honest day's labor from all of our workers, there would be no holding us back... but the trade unions are holding us back... until the grip they have on our throats is broken, the fantastic potential we have will never be realized... direct negotiation, with no intermediary, between employer and employee is the only recipe for success, as I explained to the Taoiseach last night, blah, blah, blah...*

*So there he was, a great bloated human insect, drunk on his own self-importance, puffing on his cigar and throwing back our sherry as if it were water. A cheap Cypriot sherry that I had poured into a Harvey's bottle, by the way, although he appeared not to notice my little cost saving measure. He seemed to be addressing these nuggets of eternal wisdom to Helen, as if the good news from Chicago that he was so enthusiastically broadcasting was for her alone.*

*I realized suddenly that Blake's eyes were carrying another message altogether. And that I had not seen such a glint in Helen's eyes since our wedding night. He followed her every movement shamelessly as she walked over to the side board to refill the glasses. Eilish didn't appear to give a damn. This was a game with which she was very familiar, it seemed. It was hardly worth her while to converse with a loser such as me...*

*Just then, I understood, with sudden conviction, that I was a total stranger in this company. A total stranger in my own house!*

*I mumbled some sort of excuse—but nobody was listening to me anyway—and I left them blathering away in the sitting room.*

*I made for the bedroom, where I tried to blunt the edge of my anger. I tried to direct my thoughts to other aspects of my life. Where have the dreams and noble objectives of youth gone, I asked? Those heroic deeds I was forever postponing? The countries in which I had never traveled? The languages I have never learned? The beauties I had never seduced? That delicious adultery I had never committed (though the invitation stood for over a year) and nothing was stopping me? That perfect love I had never found? That symphony I had never composed? Those books and poems that had never been read nor written? Where did they all go? All of those years? I understood now, though belatedly, that tomorrow is a day that will never arrive!*

*And that instead of pursuing the search for my own Holy Grail, I had wasted my years by playing the game of life according to rules that were drafted by Blake and his tribe. And now, as I approached my 65th year, it was too late for this Lancelot to be thinking now of uprooting himself from Camelot...*

*What fate was in store for me, then? A wallet of banknotes? Or a faux-gold watch with my name inscribed on it? Or a piece of crystal for which I have neither use nor place to put it? And the inevitable weasel words of gratitude for my years of exemplary service. Tokens of my supine loyalty to Blake, and his enterprise, over all that time! As incontrovertible proof that I recognized the peon's place I had always been destined to occupy. And that I was now willing to enjoy my well-earned suburban rest in calm tranquility until the Grim Reaper came seeking whom he might devour.*

*What will remain of me after that unwelcome event? A pale*

phantom in the minds of my erstwhile acquaintances? A ghostly presence in some amusing recollection or other? A random fragment of my idiolect that will live on after me with the guaranteed permanence of sea-foam? Who can tell? Oh God, this long lingering miserable insult they call life!

I now felt my heart hammering against my ribs like the fists of some madman hammering on the walls of his padded cell. It now seemed to me that the most basic things were being made manifest to me then for the first time ever. That dark curtains were being slowly drawn back! To reveal to me the totally empty stage that lies behind them.

I do not know what force impelled me just then to look into the bedroom mirror! Seeing myself for the first time, as it were, I noted those treacherous crow's eye wrinkles that that radiate out from the corners of my eyes, merciless timekeepers of the 40 years I have spent in the thrall of that windbag spouting his ignorant assertions downstairs.

And then, as I continue to look into the mirror, I become aware of the weird metamorphosis that now occurs. And especially of the way the contours of my face are changing right before my eyes.

Am I trying to tell you that I was becoming the werewolf of the classical horror story, replete with his sharp canine incisors and his bristling grey fur coat? Not exactly! But a more frightening metamorphosis altogether! For my image in the mirror—that odious mask of submissiveness and self-pity—was melting before my very eyes. And the wardrobe behind me was reflected in the mirror through my increasing transparency. So that all that was left of me eventually was a transparent mass bordered vaguely by the physical outline that had defined me down through the years.

Ye Gods! Could it be that I have just died? And that all that is left of me is my soul: an empty transparent vessel, filled to the brim with nothingness? Yes, at least one subservient yes-sayer has *disappeared off the face of the globe.*

*But a powerful sense of relief suffused that emptiness. Now that the hammerlock of custom has been broken, I realize that all is possible. My power can never again be denied! I realize that I can fly through the air or walk through the wall, if I so desire. And that there is no dream that I cannot make come true in real life! I exult in this belated epiphany on the road to Damascus*

*Downstairs, Helen is calling me:*

*What in God's name is keeping you up there?*

*The voice of the noxious Blake adds a footnote to her question:*

*Maybe he is getting sick... I thought he looked a bit on the pale side before he left us.*

*I realize, without a single shadow of doubt, what I must now do. Instead of answering the voices downstairs, I drag my trunk out from under our marital couch. The strength of my phantom limbs amazes me. One does not normally associate physical strength with the arms of ghosts. I quickly open the trunk, looking for what I want to find impatient fingers. It is hidden somewhere there under that mound of papers that has been accumulating with the years. Old financial statements, one or two unfinished stories, a marriage certificate, old passports, a faded birth certificate. Ah, here it is! That black leather holster I am looking for! I open it hurriedly as I hear footsteps on the bottom of the stairs. And feel the cold blue-grey steel of the Luger as it slides into the palm of my hand...*

*I hear Helen's footsteps as she reaches the landing at the top of the stairs. I had just pushed the magazine home in my pistol as she walked into the room. She seemed to see what I was about and opened her mouth to emit a shrill scream (I suppose). I fired from the hip, after the fashion of Clint Eastwood and other celluloid cowboys. The room was filled with a thunder clap that made my ears sing. My aim was perfect. The force of the impact of the bullet was such that*

*Helen's body was blown out onto the landing. I followed her out, the acrid blue smoke of the discharge as incense to my nostrils. Her staring eyes looking at me as if they were trying to solve some insoluble problem!*

*What were Blake's eyes trying to tell me as he froze, open-mouthed, half way up the stairs? To see raw fear leaping out of them was almost adequate recompense for the appalling mess I had allowed him to make of my life. Where now is that easy arrogance you affect, you shameless bastard? My bullet hit him square in the chest. Twisting around, he fell backwards down the stairs, his mouth opening and closing like a fish out of water. But whatever he was trying to say was drowned in a sudden gush of blood.*

*Do you think I wanted to hear your last testament, you thug. I placed the mouth of the Luger against his forehead and squeezed the trigger slowly and sensuously. Here is your* coup de grace, *my friend, I say, as the steel-jacketed projectile makes smithereens of his skull.*

*The screech of terror from the front door informed me that Eilish, Blake's Gorgon wife, was attempting to flee. Her hand slid down from the doorknob as my next bullet, fired into her back, finds her heart.*

*Silence reigned now in the slaughterhouse I had created. The silence of the graveyard that so well becomes the corpse-strewn scene about me! I sat down on the chair in the kitchen, placing the automatic pistol-- from whose muzzle a faint wisp of blue grey smoke was issuing--on the table in front of me.*

*What did I feel in my heart of hearts just then?*

*A sense of relief, a purity of soul, joy—if there is a single word that can encompass all of the emotions I felt, then that is exactly the word I am seeking. As if I had removed from the surface of the earth one unclean character with each bullet I fired from my Luger, that holy weapon from the armory of righteousness. I spent some time sitting there, relishing the dark force that had now risen within me, as one enjoys a drink from a spring of cold pure water as it emerges from the dark depths of a mountain.*

*Until I began to feel hunger gnawing the edge of my vitals! And please don't ask me how a phantom like me could experience the hunger of a wolf that had been starved for a week! Nor do not ask me either whither that imperious voice within me that suddenly raises a strange question that had never occurred to me before: What is stopping me from eating Blake's heart?*

*Every effort I made to push that question to the back of my mind was in vain, for it returned from such efforts with redoubled force. I have no idea why the question posed itself with such insistence.*

*Perhaps, accounts I read some years ago out of the barbarous practice that certain tribes in Papua New Guinea have of eating their enemies' hearts first gave me that strange idea. Those gentle folk were wont to roast the bodies of their slain enemies before consuming them. Since the taste of this human meat seems to resemble that of pork, according to those cannibals, such succulent fare was referred to by these gourmets as "long pig meat". Of all cuts, the heart was the most desired portion. Their belief was that the warrior who ate his enemy's heart was able to add the latter's desirable characteristics to those of his own.*

*Has this belief any valid basis?*

*I have no idea! But there is only one way to satisfy my suddenly aroused curiosity. Like a man in a dream, I rise from the table, my hand stretching towards the carving knife...*

It is here, dear neighbors that we must intervene with our censor's knife, so to speak. If only to shield you from the disgusting minor details of the carve-up perpetrated by Mr. Psycho on the bodies that lay around him.

And, worse still, from his lurid descriptions of the gourmet meals he prepared from the body parts of his erstwhile companions! The *riñones de Jerez* he prepared from the kidneys of his own wife, cooking them in the sherry that remained in the bottles in the sitting room, was but one nauseating example of his hideously grotesque cannibalism.

Not to mention that appalling barbecue to which he treated his nearby—and totally unsuspecting—neighbors. Nor the barbaric satisfaction he got from preparing those loathsome stews and soups from the bones of his victims.

The petty details of this foul butchery were so disgusting that the press and ordinary public were not allowed into the courtroom as Mr. Psycho was being cross-examined by the prosecutor.

The most outstanding aspect of Mr. Psycho's personality—much commented on by those present in the court and by the public in general—was the defendant's apparent absolute normality, both in speech and appearance. His neighbors were more than willing to tell reporters sniffing around his haunts that they had always found Mr. Psycho to be a lovely friendly sort of a fellow. This sort of person who was always willing to lend a helping hand when such was needed!

Then the Gardaí swore that the defendant had fully cooperated with them during their investigation. Indeed, it was he who had called them in the first place to draw their attention to his crime.

And was he excited or aggressive when you arrived at the scene?

On the contrary, your Honor, he was as quiet and peaceful a lamb when we arrived to apprehend him. He opened the freezer in his garage to regale us with the sight of the results of his butchery. And he apologized for the shock the sudden sight of those heads, with their open eyes staring out at us, gave all of us. As far as cooperation is concerned, your Honor, would that all defendants were as cooperative as this one! If he were younger, I don't imagine that we would have any difficulty in accepting him into the force...

His defense team put some of his acquaintances and fellow workers into the witness box where they asserted that the defendant had never exhibited any violent tendencies. This was held to demonstrate that the balance of Mr. Psycho's mind was disturbed at the time of the crime. But that now the even tenor of his calm disposition had been restored and that he was now a veritable paragon of exemplary normality. A short spell in a psychiatric facility would suffice to demonstrate that he was no longer a danger to the public.

When the jury returned from its short deliberation, they found that Mr. Psycho was indeed guilty of the heinous crime attributed to him. Although the judge claimed to have been impressed by the arguments of the defense team, he was unable, he said, to ignore the unspeakable brutality of Psycho's actions. Had the accused anything to say before he passed sentence?

The eyes of the courtroom where now on Mr. Psycho. I thank the jury for its deliberation, he said calmly, but regrettably its judgment is partly erroneous. You may well ask: why? The answer is that Brendan Blake is still alive and well! I should have driven a stake through his heart instead of eating that organ but, alas, this essential measure did not occur to me at the time. Thanks to this unforgivable negligence, a result of the pressure of circumstances that have been so graphically described in this court, our unfortunate society will still find itself subject to the dread curse of the likes of Brendan Blake.

As the courtroom digested this lunatic assertion, the crowd hardly noticed the judge announcing that he thought himself as having no other credible option than to commit Mr. Psycho to prison for life.

And this is how the same charming Mr. Psycho wound up in our care instead of being placed among ordinary convicts in one of those old-fashioned facilities, commonly called prisons.

We were amazed at first at the contradiction between the bestialities attributed to our new charge and his ready charm and civilized demeanor. He appears at breakfast every morning, spick and span, as we have said before, and with a crease in his trousers on which one could pare pencils. Already, his sound advice—especially in regard to financial matters—has been making a major contribution to the running of our establishment. His advice in regard to dealing with the trade union threat was particularly useful. One of us even commented that his detention here must have been the result of some enormous bureaucratic bungle. Indeed, she continued to hold to that opinion until she had, perforce, to read his account of the appalling butchery her charmer had perpetrated.

The search for a mask appropriate to the latter's need for systematic character reconstruction goes on here, without any sign of success so far, alas. However, as we have still to investigate the applicability of masks inspired by the wide-ranging neo-liberal pantheon to Psycho's case, we are far from despairing at finding a solution to the problem he poses us. One of our team suggested—insightfully, as it turns out—that the mask of Brendan Blake might well fit the bill, and we are continuing to explore this putative solution to our problem.

Let us remind you again, dear neighbors, that this Institute is a psychiatric facility, vulgarly known as a "prison without walls". And the possibility of a relapse to type on the part of Mr. Psycho can never be discounted.

If you have any doubts, fears or questions, do not hesitate to contact us!

In the meantime, the staff here wish you all the best and the happiest of dreams!

# THE KING'S SON

**ALL OF THIS HAPPENED** a very long time ago, and a long time ago it was. The story refers to the son of a warrior King who lived in the bleak lands of Connacht by the western ocean. And while he was young, it is related that this son never lacked for the best of food and drink, nor for the sweet music of the harp sounding from dawn to dusk. So it is related.

Nevertheless, it is also related that his heart was forever being gnawed by the fat ugly maggot of discontent. To the extent that he decided to abandon the bodily comforts he enjoyed in his father's fortress and take to wandering in foreign parts. Life must have some higher goal than satisfaction of the pleasures of table and the flesh, he said to his somewhat bemused friends.

The reputation for saintliness of Caoimhín of Glendalough, the Valley of the Two Lakes, was widely disseminated in the Ireland of his time. So, the King's son decided to cross the rivers and wooded plains of Ireland to reach the monastery of this saint in the territory of the Laighnibh. For there he would receive, he thought, the advice that would transform him, a spiritual poultice that would cure his existential malaise definitively. That is, if such a poultice really existed!

His journey eastwards through the lands of the rapacious forest dwellers of the Great Central Plain was providentially incident-free and he arrived tired, but unharmed, in the wooded valley in the Wicklow Mountains where Caoimhín's lakeside monastery was located.

To make a long story short—and a short story shorter than it arguably merits—this noble stranger was allowed access to the monastery and even  into the presence of its Abbot, Caoimhín himself. He explained, at a length and in a detail we need not emulate here, both the purpose of his journey, and the nature of his spiritual malaise, as far as he could understand it, to the wise and saintly holy man of Glendalough.

I have not the slightest belief in either God or Devil, he said. In the territory of my people Crom Dubh, that black god of the Cruach, is much venerated. But I get no longer get any solace whatsoever from veneration of that fearsome deity. Nor from the tiresome company of his faithful followers who spend hours praying and craw-thumping on the summit of his holy mountain on the annual feast day of Crom. Not to mention the mind-destroying boredom of those insipid and meaninglessly luxurious years I spent in the fortress of my father that so corroded my soul.

I would give my life, he says, to taste the reputed happiness and peace of mind that they say your God bestows on His faithful. And to bid farewell for ever to that grey discontent within rots my spirit from the inside out. If I placed myself here under your patronage, he says to Caoimhín, and if I try to stamp out every ounce of aristocratic arrogance within me, and if I go humbly on my knees before you, will you deign to give me the advice that will restore me to my full humanity?

No amount of genuflections nor self-humiliations before me—nor before the image of any deity, past or present, for that matter—will do anything to fill that emptiness you feel in your heart, says Caoimhín to this unexpected aristocratic pilgrim. Leave such empty manifestations to the demented followers of Crom Dubh, star-struck nincompoops or those many Christians, alas, who have allowed their faith to degenerate into superstition!

And let me warn you here and now that the grace of God never flows from superstition or selfish desire. But never! Work of quite another kind is needed in order to achieve that hallowed state. And believe me, it is not without attention and effort on the supplicant's part that His grace is attained. My question to you now is this: is the desire in your heart sufficiently strong to impel you to undertake whatever task I will set you?

It is known to all and sundry that you dwell in the peace of your God, oh Holy One, says the King's son. Furthermore, it is whispered among our people in the West that you earned this grace through months of prayer and fasting in a cave by the side of one of the lakes near your monastery. But, were it not for the strength of your belief in your God, you would never have been able to endure such a harsh penance. Without the help of a God in whom I do not believe, it is certain that the harshness of the penance you endured would break me... Do you think, oh Holy One, that there may be some other way to acquire the grace of your God without following the tortuous path of the solitary hermit?

Only the wisest of men could answer that question, says Caoimhín. I am not saying that such a path exists or does not exist or that it can be expressed in any of the languages of man. What I am saying is that the answer to the question depends on you alone. The question I would ask you again is this: if there were another way to achieve the peace of God, would you be willing to exert yourself, with all your might and energy, to perform the task I am about to assign you.

Of course I will be so willing, says the King's Son, if you tell me that the result would merit the effort.

I am going to ask you another question, then, says

Caoimhín.

But I am certain that it will not make any sense to you.

I am waiting to hear it, says the King's Son.

It is this, says Caoimhín. Tell me now: what is your favorite game or pastime? What are your favorite ways to while away or annul those tedious hours of boredom you so graphically described to me earlier?

The King's Son spends at few moments pondering the Saint's unexpected words. But he fails to detect any hidden reefs lurking beneath their seemingly innocuous surfaces.

I have, and have always been, a compulsive chess addict, he says.

Chess, repeats the saint, ruminatively, stroking his grey beard with long slender fingers. Hmm! Chess indeed! That gives me an interesting idea!

Suddenly he snaps his fingers, saying a short prayer under his breath, before he calls out to a cowled monk who happens to be passing by.

Go quickly, Brother Neasán, he says, and find Lomán for me. You will probably come upon him working in the vegetable garden behind the round tower. Ask him to come here immediately. And, most importantly, order him to bring one of the monastery chess sets with him.

The monk immediately sped away. And he was not long gone before they saw the aforementioned Lomán approaching, a chess board under his arm and a box containing chessmen in his hand. The King's son did not know it at the time, but Lomán was the chess champion of the monastery. It was common knowledge in this rugged corner of Ireland that no better chess player than Lomán was to be found among the men of Leinster.

Then Caoimhín entrusted another monk, Maolíosa, with bringing a sword to the spot where he and the King's son were conversing. While they were waiting for the return of this monk, Caoimhín placed the chess board on a flat rock between his visitor and Lomán and arranged the chessmen on it in their battle array.

The King's Son was not able to make any sense of this request for a sword. What has a game of chess got to do with swords, he asks himself. And, especially in the case of a living saint, whose widespread reputation for peaceful resolution of disputes was a bye-word throughout the island of Ireland? A sword is the last instrument one would associate with Caoimhín.

When the monk returned, bearing a glittering sword, Caoimhín beckoned to the two players and asked them to listen to him carefully.

Beloved Lomán, he said, what I am going to ask of you is to fulfill that vow of obedience you took as you entered this monastery for the first time. You promised that day that you would be faithful to that vow unto death. Do you still hold to that promise?

Of course I do, as God is my witness!

Well, Lomán, my brother in Christ, I am going to ask you now to play a game of chess with this youth who has come to us from the faraway region of Connacht. And if you fail to beat him, you will leave me with no choice than to behead you with this very sword.

And Caoimhín caused the quiet evening air to whistle as he then lashed it fiercely with the sword. The King's Son was amazed, and horrified, at this time of events. Were all the rumors he had heard about the sanctity of Caoimhín without foundation? Could it be that the followers of Christ where as bloodthirsty as the followers of Crom?

But, beloved brother in Christ, said Caoimhín, fair is fair. If you get the better of our visitor, let me assure you that his head will fall victim to the sharp edge of this weapon.

Once again, he fiercely lashed the evening air with the sword.

The two others looked at Caoimhín and at each other, surprise and horror in their eyes. How could they ever have imagined such an unlikely scenario? Has the saint gone mad? Could he really be serious about demanding such a bloody outcome for a simple game of chess?

However, the face of the saint was a veritable image of resolute obduracy. And, as far as the King's son was concerned, never had he failed to rise to a challenge, no matter how daunting it seemed. Nor had his people before him...

The pair, the monk and the King's Son, started to play. The latter felt beads of sweat stand out on his forehead. For, observing that sharp sword in the hands of Caoimhín, and the wild look in the saint's eyes, he understood now that his very life was genuinely at stake.

The game continued for seven days and seven nights. The advantage sometimes being with the King's Son and sometimes with Lomán! But, at the end of the week, neither player appeared to have an edge on the other.

And then, suddenly and unexpectedly, the King's Son noted a weakness, one carelessly placed pawn, in Lomán's defense. Tiredness was wreaking its toll on the monk. The Kings Son pressed his advantage home. In the blink of an eye, so to speak, he had captured the monk's Queen, a bishop and a rook. And now he placed Lomán's King under siege. One more move from his knight, and Lomán would have no escape. Checkmate, the noble visitor would proclaim triumphantly.

While Lomán was staring despairingly at the board, as he

desperately sought an escape from his plight, the King's Son began to observe him more closely. He noted a noble countenance that radiated goodness and holiness. A face that was worn and wrinkled with years of penitence and fasting, of kindness and good works!

He could hardly avoid making a comparison between the life that had been spent by Lomán and his own wasted years. On the enemies he had slaughtered brutally and wantonly, on the nihilistic blandishments of the alehouse! On the satisfaction of greedy lusts that were nothing more nor less than cynical imitations of love. And, above all, that accursed boredom that left a sour taste of ashes in his mouth.

He felt a great wave of shame, as it were, well up from the depths of his mind. And when it broke on the shoals of his consciousness, it left a residue in the form of a firm resolve behind it. Along with an overwhelming sense of pity in his heart for his opponent!

He now knew what he had to do, in spite of the price he knew he would have to pay for such an act. He made a deliberately stupid move. Lomán seized his opportunity to escape from the quandary in which his opponent's skill had placed him. He could scarcely believe his luck as the King's Son made a mistake after stupid mistake. Until the advantage the latter had so patiently constructed disappeared like a will o' the wisp. And now the Connacht man's King was left without any defense that could withstand Lomán's onslaught...

Caoimhín had been following the game closely from its beginnings. Now, and without a word of warning, he stretched out his hand and swept both chessmen and board from the stone flag onto the ground. The two players sat there, open-mouthed. Not knowing what to say.

The saintly Caoimhín then broke the silence.

This is a game that will never be won, nor lost, he said

slowly, emphasizing every word. No head will be cut off here by this sword today nor ever. And then, addressing himself to the Kings son, he said: two things only are demanded of the supplicant who desires to receive the grace of God: the full commitment of his heart, and love for his neighbor. You have shown both of these blessed traits during the game you have just played. You committed yourself fully to the game in order to save your own life.

Nevertheless, you demonstrated that there is a higher place yet in your heart for that pearl without price, the willingness to sacrifice your life for that of your neighbor. Therefore, I have no reservation about inviting you to spend some time with us. Show the same love and commitment to our discipline here and I promise you that you will soon feel your heart alight with the love of God.

And will I get then to feel the presence of your God in my heart, asked the King's Son.

Caoimhín looked at the young visitor, somewhat surprisedly, before speaking:

His sacred presence, may He be praised for ever, he said, has already made itself manifest to you. And for that let us say hallelujah and hosanna in the highest and a fervent prayer of thanksgiving...

# SEAN-NÓS (*THE OLD STYLE)*

**NOTHING WORSE** than a wet Sunday, *compadre*!

No sir! Since you got up this blessed morning, you have spent your day slouched in that armchair. Motionless! Hardly stirring out of it! Yep! Deep in your brown study! Gazing at patterns the raindrops make as they trickle down the windows of your apartment. Wondering: are these patterns pure random formations, the limitless faces of chaos? Or can they or life itself (if it comes to that) be synchronous with the expression of some transcendental intentionality whose nature we can never know?

The words of the erudite Charles Sherrington, who famously describes the brain in 1917 as "an enchanted loom where millions of flashing shuttles weave a dissolving pattern, always a meaningful pattern, though never an abiding one" float inconsequentially in and out of my mind.

Always meaningful? Ever purposeful? Never abiding! The pattern of those raindrops?

Forget such pointless lunatic meanderings, Bernard, on a day such as this!

Consider the concrete: that missive in its cheap brown envelope, for example. With its Irish postage stamp affixed upside down. It arrived, unannounced, in your postbox on Friday.

Containing nothing but a cutting from the *Connacht Herald* bearing the signature S. Ó L. scrawled carelessly with red biro ink!

Who is S. Ó L? Some Seán or other? Or Séamas, Seathrún, Somhairle, or Seosamh? Or Siobhán, Sorcha, Sinéad, or Sadhbh? Possibly, as the use by women of the masculine form of Gaelic patronymics, replacing the traditional Uí, has become commonplace since you shook the dust of Ireland off your feet. And that Ó L? Ó Lachtnáin, Ó Lafartaigh, Ó Laoi, Ó Laoide, Ó Laoire, Ó Laighléis, Ó Liatháin, Ó Lochlainn, Ó Loideáin, Ó Lonagáin, Ó Lonargáin, Ó Lorcáin, Ó Luain, Ó Luanaigh, Ó Luasa, Ó Lupáin? All of these could designate either man or woman.

You consider all possibilities among the officially designated genders. For all the good that does you! You then read a short article describing how Mrs. Maura Griffin, known widely as Máire Jude Shéamais, lost her life in a road accident near her home in Ardaun. It seems that she was knocked down by a car as she returned from the post office. The driver of the vehicle in question, alleged to have been drunk at the time of the accident, is to be charged shortly with her manslaughter.

In this clipping, the life and work of Máire Jude Shéamais, one of Ireland's foremost traditional singers, is briefly described. The number of Oireachtas prizes she had won! The concerts in which she had participated, at home and abroad! The cassettes and CDs of her characteristic style of singing! The others that had been planned but for her untimely death! *Bean an Fhir Rua* (The Wife of the Red-haired Man) recorded in Boston, her own unique version of *An Droighneán Donn* (The Blackthorn Bush) recorded in Paris... Her husband, Mícheál, and her five children, three sons and two daughters, are heartbroken at their loss. *Cór Chúil Aodha* (the Coolea Choir) is to sing at her Requiem Mass, with traditional singers from all over the country expected to be in attendance.

The funeral would have been well over by the time this mystery S. Ó L's missive has arrived, of course. The body of Máire Jude Shéamais is now making clay in Ardaun churchyard!

Who sent you that information? And how did he, or she, know your address, given that you have broken all links with the homeland and have been scarcely a year in your present accommodation. How did he, or she, even know that you were still alive?

And, above anything else:  how did this mysterious messenger know that you, Bernard, would be interested in—*recte*, engrossed, if the full truth is to be known—by the story of the death of Máire Jude Shéamais?

What really grips you, though, is that photograph of Máire Jude Shéamais in that newspaper clipping. And you thought that that wound had healed itself a long time ago. Even if the scar it left in your soul had not been fully effaced by time!

For, you, Bernard, cannot see a smiling middle-aged housewife in that photograph.

That smile, as far as you are concerned, belongs to that lithe young woman who walked hand-in-hand with you along a starlit Coral Strand, in a far-distant dusk of early summer. You still feel the warmth of her skin beneath the palm of your hand. And you marvel at its silky softness as you introduce your fingers under her light cotton blouse. You had read about such smoothness, of course, in the various novels you had browsed to relieve the stress of your studies. But this was the first time you had ever experienced it alive beneath your touch. Pure silk!  And the miracle: she did not thrust your hand away from her. That wordless conversation between you as gleaming moonlit coral crunches beneath our tread...

You still, many years afterwards, feel the pressure of her arm about your waist, Bernard, the small waves of the ebb-tide hissing weakly on the fluorescent shingle beneath you. The lonely call of seabirds out on the deep, moon and stars hanging from the invisible rafters of space-time, the mingled perfume of ocean and rotting littoral algae in your nostrils.

You remember, as if it was yesterday, that pint you drank later beside her in the Coral Strand Hotel. The bar was crowded, both with local residents and visitors like yourself. How proud you felt then. Without the slightest exaggeration, for natural grace, not one of those fancy stuck-up college belles could hold a candle to Máire.

That was your first pint of stout ever, Bernard. But you never admitted such a flaw in your manliness to Máire. You were twenty years old then and had never before appreciated the creaminess of a well-drawn pint. It would be difficult for an Ardaun woman such as Máire to appreciate the virtues of total abstinence or, even, to believe that such were possible. But Ardaun was not Dublin! This was another life altogether. And although that pint was the first of many, its taste will always remain on your tongue.

No point in denying, either, that your eyes are still enthralled by the deep sea-blue eyes of Máire Jude Shéamais, her warm breath still in your ear as she whispers:

I'll bet that you have a steady girl-friend up there in Dublin, Bernard!

For a few moments you brought to mind Irene, the TD[7]'s daughter, that sodality girl who wouldn't allow your tongue to probe beyond her tightly-clenched teeth. Because such "messing" outside the bond of marriage is a mortal sin, as she so tartly informed you. You now let the image of Irene be swept away in the undertow of a fast-ebbing tide.

If that was true once, Máire, it has become a part of the past tense since I have become yours, you say with your utmost sincerity.

And that was nothing but the truth at the time you said it…

The visitors at the bar were clamoring to hear 'a local song' since technical difficulties, excess of Guinness or memory lapse—or these three factors working in connivance—had brought an abrupt ending to a somewhat tuneless version of *England's Motorway* in the middle of the third verse, being raucously belted out in a snug beside the counter. The hoarse porter-drenched voice of a Dubliner could then be heard to say:

None of yer oul' 'Galway Bay' come-all-yes now, lads! If you ever go across the sea to Ireland sort of shite! Le's have the rale McEye now. Th'oul Gaelic, lads, de rale ting, a par' o' wha' we are…

Another voice sounds from the center of the crowd: Máire Jude Shéamais is somewhere around here. I saw her coming in a

7 *Teachta Dála – member of the Irish parliament*

short while ago. Ask her to give a stave[8] of the 'rale McEye', if that's what ye want. She's the girl to give it to ye. If only to put a *gobán*[9] in that Jackeen's mouth!

What Máire Jude Shéamais are you talkin' about, Cóilí?

The wan from Ardaun that does be singin' on the radio! Don't you see her over there in the corner cosying up to that long-haired student who is stayin' over in Mannions?

And a fine cut of a wan she is too! An' me thinkin' that nothing good ever came out of Ardaun, that shithole, but periwinkles and the odd truss of seaweed.

Oh, the devil take it! I thought I'd be safe around here, thinking that nobody from these parts would recognize me, whispers Máire into my ear. I'd be ashamed to open my mouth in this place, where singers grow on bushes.

But the popular clamor for a song from the linnet of Ardaun cannot be denied.

Máire rises, leaves my side and walks to the centre of the bar. Your eyes follow her figure as she disappears among the throng. Strong shapely calves and long jet-black hair that reaches down to the small of her back! Many other male and jealous female eyes follow the sway of her slender waist and full hips.

I have really fallen on my feet tonight, you say to yourself.

The crowd around Máire continues to talk and drink. You get a glimpse of her again in their midst. She sees you looking at her and stares directly at you. A long longing look that reaches right into your very soul...

She then shuts her eyes and starts to sing. Her voice is scarcely audible at first. But as the people beside her fall silent she gradually increases the volume of her delivery until the silence of the listeners stretches as far as the bar itself. Men stare into their pints, their glasses of whiskey, at the ceiling, in utter silence. For, it is understood—albeit mistily—that the song they now hear has

---

[8] *a verse of a song*
[9] *gag*

herded them into the presence of the ineffable! Into a zone where the bonds that confine us to the real have been loosed and other possibilities make themselves manifest. It seemed to you, Bernard, that Máire's voice fixed hitherto unsuspected wings to the souls of all who were listening to her. To yours included! And that song has been echoing in your head ever since.

It is a version of *Casadh an tSúgáin* (The Twisting of the Rope) that you had never heard before. Nor anybody else in that company, for that matter! Imposing a slower rhythm than is usual for this song, Máire introduced extra grace notes into it, extra flourishes that elevated this simplest of folk songs to a higher artistic dimension.She opens her eyes and looks directly at you, Bernard, when she reaches the final chorus of the song. With a gaze that, once again, penetrates and interrogates the very depths of your soul!

> *If you are with me, be with me,*
> *o bright love of my heart;*
> *If you are with me, be with me,*
> *by day and by night;*
> *If you are with me, be with me,*
> *to the last inch of your heart*
> *My sorrow and desolation*
> *that you are not now my woman.*

When she reaches the end of the song, the bar remains silent after the dying of the last note. As if people didn't wish to leave the magical zone that had been created. But when they finally emerge from this enchantment, the shouts of praise and the handclapping almost raise the roof.

When she returns to sit on the chair beside you, and when you put your arm around her shoulders, you notice that the back of her blouse is drenched in perspiration.

Was that really *The Twisting of the Rope*? I do not claim to be an expert in these matters, you said to her, but that is the first time I have ever heard that version of the song.

You never heard it before nor will you ever hear it again, Bernard. It surged out, red-hot, from the very depths of my heart. Uninvited and unsought, so to speak! I am certain that I could never sing it again. Just let me say that this is the gift I bring to you. Have you a gift to bring to me?

It is then you make your solemn promise.

### 2.

In the train, as you return to Dublin. Your head is a maelstrom of confused thoughts. Still, you decide to keep that solemn promise you made in the Coral Strand Hotel. You will leave your home, with all of its attendant comforts, immediately. To spend the rest of your life with Máire Jude Shéamais! 'Be with me to the last inch of your heart', wasn't that what she begged of you? Her message underlined by the entreaty in those deep blue eyes in which you imagined the blue of the sky and the blue of the sea in perpetual contention.

But, to give you your due, you never allow your heart to take complete control of your impulses, Bernard. Neither then or ever! Some call it cowardice, others common sense...

The subtle voice of reason, of this plain common sense, now battles to be heard. It addresses itself conspiratorially to you as the train passes through Ballinasloe:

Consider your position, Bernard! You are only in your second year at the university. With two years of intensive studies still in front of you, before they award you that blessed piece of paper! In the meantime you subsist, penniless, except for that pittance you earn working weekends as a relief barman in the *Hare and Hounds*. No, Bernard, it is time to face up to your grim reality: for your keep you are absolutely dependent on your parents.

As the train crosses the Shannon just before reaching Athlone, realism beats a retreat as the heart counter-attacks: No worthwhile decision was ever made that didn't involve some element of risk, it says. And isn't work available always in England and America for willing hands? And you do have a strong pair of arms. Surely you could earn the staff of life for both of you with the sweat of your brow?

You remember, just then, the shame you felt at your mother's tears when you communicated to your parents that you had no vocation for the priesthood. All those novenas she had made and rosaries said so that Our Lord above would not give the deaf ear to her entreaty! To have a son a priest would crown her motherhood!

You could hardly imagine the extent of her anguish on receiving a letter from you one fine day. From Boston or Birmingham, say! In which she would read that the apple of her eye had been stolen from her by some woman she had never even met and whose people were unknown to her. A people—to make matters infinitely worse—without any social standing whatsoever! Who live on the edge of some god-awful bog, in the back of beyond, in some stony poverty-stricken parish in the remote West of Ireland! Did she deserve such a calamitous let-down, Bernard, after all the prayers and rosaries she had said on your behalf?

As the train glides between the broad green plains of Kildare's horse country, right reason intensifies its counter-attack on the lucubrations of the heart:

After all the sacrifices your parents have made on your behalf, surely you are obliged—if only out of filial gratitude—never to say or do anything that might hurt them as long as they are in the land of the living. After all we have sacrificed for you, Bernard, is this all the thanks we get?

The fact that these considerations are shot through with images of Máire Jude Shéamais, her face bathed in moonlight as you both walk along the shingle of the Coral Strand, adds to your confusion. Along with her haunting '*If you are with me, be really with me, to the last inch of your heart*' sounding in the echoing chambers of your brain. And you, sifting through all of these confused images of past and future, vainly try to locate the one true spur to action.

You try to sweep these images and argument out of your mind by recalling aspects of the Theory of Relativity you memorized for your latest Physics test at the university. Let the clarity of Einstein sweep away all this confusion, you said, Bernard! And speak now out of that clarity, conscience!

But all you can hear was Máire Jude Shéamais singing the chorus of *The Twisting of the Rope!*

To add to your confusion, Bernard, those letters started to arrive. And, in a way, the same letters made your decision for you. One letter per week from her, at least! And sometimes much more frequently! The childishness of her writing surprised you. It appeared to be so much out of synch with the magisterial elegance of her singing. You didn't know what to make of these inelegantly scrawled missives.

Your ever-vigilant mother wants to know why this child is writing to you from somewhere down the country. A child! If she knew the half of it! Thankfully, Máire writes neither her name nor address on the envelopes of her letters and your mother hasn't a word of Gaelic. For, if she could gauge the content of these "childish" letters, then the shit would surely hit the fan, as they say. Tons of it!

Why don't you bring one of your girl classmates home one of these days, your mother asks you often, these days. Now that the priesthood issue has been well and truly buried, virtue must be made of necessity. And always with a parvenu's hope to God that you will manage to introduce the daughter of some banker or doctor or similar member of the respectability into the household.

So, she purred like a cat that has just been presented with a bowl of cream, the day you brought Irene of the clenched teeth, daughter of a government Minister, to the house. Even if the latter's politics were not in line with those of your household, Bernard, the social acceptability of his daughter was unquestionable!

That was a good move, son, said your father, at breakfast the following morning. Keep in with that crowd, that's my advice to you. Keep always close to where the power is and you'll never put a foot wrong!

When all is said and done, you understand completely, Bernard, that presenting Máire Jude Shéamais to such parents would be akin to presenting to them a black woman from Timbuktu. Apart from that, Máire's low standard of formal education sounds other warning bells.

Remember that she told you once that she went to work as a skivvy in a hotel in Galway soon after she had completed her primary education. You paid no attention to that snippet of information at the time. Once the initial infatuation had burned itself out (although you found such an eventuality somewhat incredible) it would be *de rigeur* for the long-term happiness of any couple, that both partners be culturally on a par with each other and, thereby, share common interests. Or so you read somewhere, Bernard, in a newspaper article that appeared to you to make sound common sense.

Keep a grip on yourself, Bernard, then! Subject the wayward impulses of your heart, and those deep blue eyes, to the discipline of sound reason!

It was just about then that you ceased answering those letters with their embarrassingly childish calligraphy.

Years afterwards, you read in the *Connacht Herald* that the famous traditional singer, Máire Ní Chlochartaigh (Cloherty) wed the well-known local contractor and Manager of Ardaun Gaels' football team, Páraic Ó Gríofa (Griffin). The reception was held in the Coral Beach Hotel...

The aspect of that report that turned that white-hot knife in your flesh, Bernard, was the information that the bride sang her much-commented-on individual version of *The Twisting of the Rope* at the wedding breakfast.

### 3.

You tell Neus, successor of Laia, successor of Nùria successor of that egregious Gorgon, Irene, that you become nauseous in supermarkets—with the dreaded and incurable shopping sickness— and the silly creature believes you. The cynical manipulations of races that have lived for centuries under the boot are poorly understood by those that have not...

So, while the week's vegetables are being purchased by Neus in La Boquería, just off La Rambla, you are off the leash here in the center of Barcelona. You have arranged to meet her later in the Café Zürich, on the corner of the Plaza de Catalunya that faces La Rambla, in about an hour's time. It is one of those perfect days for strolling: a clear blue sky above, a gentle heat in the sunlight tempered by the delicious coolness of a easterly breeze from the Mediterranean. You may decide on a leisurely amble up the Rambla towards the statue of Colón and the port area behind it. There to lazily survey the moored craft before returning to the Plaza to meet Neus. Or you could simply sip a long cool *Estrella*, the local beer, outside the Café Zürich, simultaneously browsing through the newspaper, to see what latest tricks the local politicos are pulling.

As you pause there indecisively, you notice a small booth on the edge of the wide footpath of the Plaza. A swarthy elderly woman with long black hair, wearing large golden earrings sits inside it. A lady of the *raza Gitana*, an Andalucian gypsy, without doubt! An empty chair is parked in front of her booth. You scan the words on the star-spangled multicolored sign over the booth:

*Love... Job... Money... Health*

### WHAT DOES THE FUTURE HAVE IN STORE ?

*OUR TAROT CARDS*

*CAN READ YOUR FATE*

### 5 EUROS

You, Bernard, incorrigible rationalist that you are, have no interest whatsoever in any species of magical thinking. Astrological charts, healing crystals, witchcraft, haruspexy, Kabbalah, the I Ching, magic mantras, Tibetan prayer flags and that whole burgeoning faux-Asian pot-pourri of New Age superstition and assorted forms of navel-gazing signal the terminal decline of the Age of Enlightenment. They are the rot at the core of the apple, as far as you are concerned. And as regards fortune telling based on the Tarot, please don't get me started!

So, you tell yourself, this booth is undoubtedly a machine designed to extract easy pickings from the pockets of tourists, the metaphysically confused and the irremediably naive.

But whatever whim, spasm of idle curiosity, perverse subliminal nudge or just plain boredom, impels you, suddenly you find yourself sitting down on that chair in front of that gypsy lady. If indeed 'gypsy' she be. You slap your 5€ note on the table in front of her. Avoiding your eyes, it seems, she stuffs the money into the battered leather purse that is hanging around her neck. She then picks up the pack of cards on the table and automatically begins to cut it.

'Love, job, money or health?' she intones, still without looking at you.

As if she were scrutinizing the cards intently, her forehead scrunched up in wrinkles! She has performed this rite mechanically thousands of times before this...

I would like to know something about my life that is broader than any one of those aspects! And since the word "Fate" is up there on your sign, I thought that...

Fate is broader, as you say, and more complicated than any one of its aspects, she of the earrings says. To investigate it fully, I will also have to read your palm. And that will cost you another 5 Euros.

You are crazy, Bernard. You know full well that this is shameless robbery. But, curiosity overcomes your good sense and you fork out. You are not in the mood for haggling over the price. You slap down another 5 Euro note on the table in front of her as she continues to murmur while shuffling her cards.

What is your Christian name, she then asks.

Bernardo, you say.

And your star sign?

How would I know that, you say, when I never took any interest in superstitions.

She laughs lightly, the movements of her face setting her earrings dancing.

We all live by some superstition, *cariño*. The question is: which superstition? All I need to know is your birthday.

The 12th of March, then!

Good! That means that you are a Pisces. That is very helpful. That is my star sign also, and the cards speak to me with total clarity when a customer shares my sign.

She continues shuffling the cards, staring at them as if concentrating on them, as she continues to intone 'Bernardo... Pisces... his Fate... Bernardo... Pisces... his Fate' in a low monotonous monotone! Then she stops suddenly and proceeds to lay out the cards, one after the other, in a complicated pattern, approximating at first to a cross, on the table. She remains staring at them for a long interval, saying nothing. You begin to lose your patience.

Well, what do you think?

I think nothing, sir. I am simply a medium through which the cards say what only can be said. But let me tell you that you did... something, well, extremely negative, let us say, happened to you in your youth. Your life ever since has deviated from its true course...

Is that so? Could you be a little more specific? Could it be that you are referring to the profession that I chose, for example?

The cards are telling me here, as clear as the light of day, that this negativity and whatever bad luck flowed from it is, as almost always, connected with an affair of the heart... Let me look now at the palm of your hand to see if we can get further clarification!

What a fool you are, Bernard! Dabbling in superstition this fine clear morning in the 21$^{st}$ century! In the center of a quintessentially modern city! After reading in your morning newspaper about the moons of Titan, planned expeditions to Mars and the exotic possibilities of human cloning! But so what! This journey into the speculative realm kills time and boredom as you wait for Neus with her vegetables. Chalk it all up as human experience! So you place your right hand, palm upwards, on the table. The gypsy spends some time scrutinizing it, her eyes darting back and forth between it and the cards. The wrinkles on her brow deepen.

Well?

Your palm and the cards tell me that something unique happened to you, a thing that happens to very few on the surface of this globe. The Fates privileged you to meet the person they had chosen for you to be your life's companion. Such an incredible offer demands a corresponding responsibility...

Meaning???

When the Fates' bounty is refused, a disordered life and much unnecessary suffering are the inescapable consequences. They never forgive he who refuses to follow the path that they have chosen for him. The cards and your palm indicate that you refused to abandon your comfortable lifestyle for the unique opportunity vouchsafed you by the Fates. Both your own life and that of the life companion they chose for you have suffered ever since the consequences of this refusal.

But, how can you be so certain that what you say is true? Maybe you have misread...

The evidence of the cards and of your own palm, sir, is unambiguous. It never lies.

At first I am disturbed, by such a "revelation". But, on reflection, wasn't the gypsy's description of my life so general that she could read the life of anyone else in the same way?

Appearing to read my thoughts, this strange soothsayer then says:

The Tarot cards never fall in a random pattern, sir. Chance is never involved. Ever! Apart from what I have just told you, they tell me that you sought solace in the arms of other women. But that you superimposed the face of the one chosen for you by the Fates over the faces of her successors. In this way, you did them a grave injustice. You yourself suffer! For the person who has been granted the right to travel on life's main highway is never satisfied with mean and sordid laneways. The distractions of those laneways may keep the worm of discontent asleep in the heart of the person who betrays the trust of the Fates. But these distractions have sell-by dates: that worm always awakens...

But, how about what life has in store for me, for which I paid my 10 Euros? Where is all of this "ill-luck" you talk about going to lead me?

Let me tell you the whole truth in a few words, sir! When you turned your back on that love, you threw down your gauntlet to the Fates. And, if you don't mind, I would rather terminate this session right now, she says, gathering up the cards from the table and re-organizing them in a pack. But don't be worried, *cariño*; I'll give you your money back.

And, unbelievably, she takes your 5 Euro note out from the leather purse hanging around her neck, adds it to the other note that is still on the table, and offers you the two notes with a graceful movement of her hand.

Please, take this back, she says.

But tell me why you don't want to continue your soothsaying, you say, accepting the proffered shekels.

Go from this place, Bernardo, believing that the message of the cards you heard through me was nothing but lies. And that you really don't want to spend your money to hear me read you the rest of that message!

The message of the Tarot lady, especially the part she refused to divulge, continued to exercise your imagination for some time, Bernard. What, if anything, was she hiding from you? In order answer these questions, you paid repeated visits to that the precise spot, up the Plaza de Catalunya from the Café Zurich, where that Tarot booth was located! But it had appeared to have vanished without trace. One of the café waiters tells you that such a booth could never have been erected there.

If, indeed, it had ever existed anywhere! Maybe that gypsy soothsayer and her booth were mere creatures of your own imagination.

### 4.

Deep in your brown study, Bernard! Gazing at the patterns the raindrops make as they trickle down the windows of your apartment. Are these patterns random configurations, born of absolute chaos, you ask yourself.

Or do they, or life itself (if it comes to that), conform to some transcendental order whose nature we can never know? Or, whence now this sudden apprehension of an occult Jungian synchronicity conforming to an unsuspected rationality that subtends and transcends the boundaries of all perceived reality, the limits of all mundane reason?

To aid your escape from this unexpected glimpse of a dizzying, disturbing, perspective, it suddenly occurs to you, apropos of nothing, that you have secreted, somewhere in your apartment, an old cassette, *The Best Songs of Máire Jude Shéamais*. But where exactly is it? It is years, aeons, since you last subjected yourself to the bitter self-recrimination that that voice always carries in its train. Little pleasure comes from rubbing salt into open wounds.

But now that the singer is dead and her enchantment is, hopefully, no more, what better way to mourn her—together with your own botched life—than to listen to her unique version of the *Twisting of the Rope* once again. For the last time, Bernard, definitely for the last time! Then you will destroy that cassette, stamp repeatedly on it to break it into smithereens. Thus you will lay the ghost that has been haunting you for years, ever since that fateful encounter in Ardaun, finally to rest.

Your mind confirms this decision and you rise up from your chair. The sudden movement after so much inaction sets stars dancing before your eyes. You switch on the light to counteract the gathering gloom of dusk. You walk stiffly, stretching and yawning, towards the bottom shelf where you keep your music cassettes and DVDs. You hunker down to better access your hoard, blowing dust off cassettes to reveal the notes that describe their contents. Joe Heaney, Caitlín Maude, Seán 'ac Dhonnchadha... and other master exponents of an art whose enchantments you have sedulously avoided for years now.

At last your fingers encounter the cassette you are seeking:

### MÁ BHÍONN TÚ, LIOM BÍ LIOM

*If you love me, really love me*

### Cnuasach d'Amhráin ón Ardán

*A Collection of Songs from Ardaun*

### Á gcasadh ar an tsean-nós ag Máire Jude Shéamais

*Sung in the traditional manner by Máire Griffin*

You found it at the bottom of the pile, of course! That same label...That slight half-rueful smile, those big sad eyes that seem, with your superheated historical imagination, to reflect the suffering of generations. And how damn well they do just that, imagination be damned! The eyes and the face of a broken people you have spent half a lifetime vainly trying to expunge from your memory!

You make for the fridge, Bernard, with that cassette in your hand. You pull its door open and tear a green can of beer out of the six-pack nesting there on the uppermost shelf. Voll Damm, Double Malt, 7.2%! You snap off the flip-top, raise the can to your lips and feel that long cold draught filter down into your innards. You then compose your mind to bid farewell to the long souring of youth's dream.

You fit the tape into the cassette player and press the start button. Sitting back again in your battered armchair, you shut your eyes and let that voice and those songs you haven't heard for eons open the doors of your imagination.

No sooner do you hear that angelic voice, than the ephemeral furniture of your present life, the very Raval itself, vanishes from sight. The mysterious alchemy of a voice, pure as mountain spring water, transports you back to another reality.

You sit once again in the bar of the Coral Strand Hotel, that night of the promise when the singer dedicated her version of *The Twisting of the Rope* to you, Bernard. To you alone! A version that you will never hear again outside the echo-chamber of your own tortured memories! You sink another long sensuous draught from your beer can, as you listen to the song Máire now sings:

> Don't bury me in Leitir Caladh;
> There here lie none of my people,
> But take me westwards to Mweenish,
> For it is there I'll be truly keened,
> Light will dance on the sand-dunes there
> And loneliness I'll never feel...

Suddenly you ask yourself: has the recording become corrupted. For, you hear a strange noise welling up behind the song.

Morphing into the noise of a crowd behind the singer, as it were, muffled voices intent on drowning out her song. You listen more carefully. Is that a living woman crying? Or is it the voice of a banshee keening the dead? Behind the song and that chilling wail, you can hear the buzz of the voices of men and women.

Other voices join the chorus reawaken long buried memories. The voices of friends and acquaintances consigned by you to the realms of forgetfulness! Of parents and relatives who expected your conformity to their *mores* on the basis of some fancied mystical quality of blood relatedness. The reproachful voices of women to whom you gave the face of Máire Jude Shéamais! The bitter reproachful voice of Irene! Priests talk to you solemnly about the wages of sin and the solace offered by Holy Mother Church! A woman's voice reads your autobiography from the palm of your hands and a deck of Tarot cards on the Plaza de Catalunya!

A strange thought suddenly chills you. Am I listening now to the voices of the dead and the imagined? To a ghostly chorus behind the sand dunes of Mweenish?And now the voice you then hear sends cold shivers coursing up and down your spine, raises the hair on the back of your neck.

Máire Jude Shéamais is speaking!

The din in your head condenses itself into that phantom voice speaking about that cowardice that erodes and rots the human fiber. Is she is speaking directly to you? Yes! Our space-time matrix vanishes like a puff of smoke.

> *If you are with me,*
> *Bernard, be really with me,*
> *Be with me to the last inch of your heart.*

You sense her presence in the room here, the fleeting warmth of her body beneath your fingertips, the softness of her lips grazing your lips, her soft tongue thrusting like a live fish against your tongue, the perfume of seaweed in your nostrils. The lights of the Raval flick on, one after the other. Night falls slowly...

You sit here, unmoving, Bernard, still hearing the dying notes of that song. The silence of the apartment now is the same silence that fell on the crowded bar of The Coral Beach Hotel just after Máire Jude Shéamais sang her version of *The Twisting of the Rope.*

> *Don't bury me in Leitir Caladh,*
> *To where I'll be truly keened,*
> *Light will dance on the sand-dunes there;*
> *Loneliness I'll never feel...*

These words seem to erupt, Bernard, from the darkness of your own soul. As if that 'last inch of your heart', that you denied Máire Jude Shéamais, has found now its corresponding form of words and action.

Every raindrop that trickles down that window in front of you is now an actor in a drama that was already written before time began. Its birth, journey and final disappearance are defined by that script. A script that tells you unequivocally the actions and gestures that will now accompany your own lines in this drama.

You now know what you must do.

For, the urge to feel the darkness outside on your skin is overpowering. You need to taste it in your mouth. To have its black stink fill your nostrils, its soundless symphony fill your ears. To be with her to the last inch of your heart! Forever...

You reach for your jacket, Bernard, and put it on mechanically, like a man in a dream.

You tear that cutting from the *Connacht Herald* up into little pieces that you let fall through your fingers to the floor.

You then walk towards the door.

Your keys rest on the table.

You leave them lying there.

# DIARY OF AN ANT

**YOU ARE AWAKE,** o Phantom mine!

You never leave me. Even if you do live in a remote cave of my imagination! I hear your request and place this empty page here in front of us. The scratching of my pen bares my soul. Follow that sound with an attentive ghostly ear...

Almost 5 pm in Hormiga Tower. Those office clock hands, vigilantly watched by our staff, will only be erased from my soul with my dying breath. From the great window:

A red sun sets through smog behind that famous Megalopolis skyline, beloved of film directors.

Lights flick on—singly and in banks—in that darkening mass of buildings.

Dusk thickens in the great canyons below, made frenetic by leaping neon signs. First stars blink from a cobalt sky.

A giant statue in the harbor's eastern approaches, its torch held aloft, melts into the dusk.

Sudden floodlighting guards it from drowning in the night's dark tides.

Traffic far below me emits its habitual distant hum.

Impatient car horns draw hellish echoes from these concrete canyons.

Police helicopters monitor traffic, clatter between buildings.

As on any other Friday here in Hormiga Tower, our Kingdom of the Bland...

Hormigans scurry to and fro as they prepare to abandon the nest. Or so they think. The nest's horizons are much broader than they can ever imagine.

Hormiga Tower is everywhere.

Their imagined escape from Hormiga Tower colonizes the brains of these Hormigans. Golf, if the good weather holds? A swim in the warm relaxing waters of the country club? All within the walls of Hormiga Tower! 'Have-a-good-weekend' flies back and forth as the Hormigans abandon the office. It flies in my direction also. For I am also a Hormigan. So they still think. However, if they suspected our joint existence, Phantom, we would hardly top the popularity poll in Hormiga Tower.

Give that leper a bell, Hormigans would say.

No kindly disposition ferments behind those smiling Hormigan masks. If our symbiosis became known, they would swear:

*that I am unconventional*

*that I am insane*

*that I merit expulsion*

*that I should be in a psychiatric hospital*

*in a prison*

*in a cemetery*

You would detect the sneer behind my back. The knowing eye winking, unseen by me. Birds recognize the presence of interlopers from other species in their midst. And act on that understanding with their sharp grey beaks, with their rending tearing claws

*Stick to the Hormigan metaphor!* you tell me Phantom? *Myrmecology texts says Hormigans cannibalize wounded comrades.* Okay! No more birds!

You already know that I despise Hormigan culture and thought. Or do you really think that Hormiganism, being based on lies and predigested opinions fed to them by our Hormigan Masters, merits the label 'thought'?

*Hormiganism?*

For example, Hormigans believe that Hormiga Tower itself is founded on a mysterious secret that transcends the ability of Hormigans to understand it. Some transcendental I hidden hand.

—We don't need to understand this secret, say Hormigans to your face.

—Of course you don't, respond the Masters. Why even try to understand it! Why not forget it altogether! Your part of our bargain, say the Masters to us, is simply to affirm the existence of that secret. That is all. And to base your comfy life in this Hormiga Tower on that affirmation.

This 'bargain' hypnotizes right-thinking Hormigans. So they never even think to look for the real motive behind the mission of Hormiga Tower.

Oh, I know what you are thinking, Phantom. But let me answer you before you open your mouth, if I may speak metaphorically.

Don't be fooled by the dilatory ways of Hormigans, by the little tricks they play on the upper echelons of the Hormiga Tower hierarchy, even by their idleness when the Master is away. But, try to tell these Hormigans the real mystery on which our nest is founded! It is then, my dear Phantom, that you will be most unpleasantly surprised by the propensity of Hormigans to cannibalize their kind.

*So, why is the sense of Hormigan existence hidden so?*

Well, Phantom: to understand that, please note the following:

If Hormigans discovered the secret of their nest, they would awake from the Great Hormigan Sleep!

Consider the implications, my ghostly friend! With Hormigan scales removed from their eyes, awakened Hormigans would discover that they were no longer Hormigans. *Ipse facto*, they would be freed from their subjection to Hormigan discipline. No-one knows what such ex-Hormigans would be capable of, what strange notions might occur to them. We have precedents that are hardly encouraging.

*Why then my daily homage before the unholy altars of Hormiga House?*

Sometimes I wonder, Phantom, if underneath their masks, many Hormigans understand the secret, just like me, but nevertheless decide to play the Hormigan game as cynically as I do. Groundless speculation of course. We'll never know. And we are all subject to one brutal fact of life! Lies feed us. Hypocrisy lubricates life's torpid machinery.

Our very language describes life as *slí na bréige* [10]?

And so: my absurd daily charade in Hormiga Tower.

Your interjections, Phantom, interrupt my story. I thought you were madly enthused to hear it. But, instead, you tangle me in a web of abstractions. Now, where were we?

---

[10]  *the way of lies*

2.

Five o clock, says the office clock. Why hang around longer! I descend to the street, where a touch of frost is promised by the light westerly breeze up from the river. Fall's leavings—the few bedraggled leaves on trees in the park opposite our tower—flaunt a defiantly festive red. Melted red gold layers itself generously on the summits of the giant towers of Megalopolis. 'Dull would he be of soul who could pass by a sight so touching in its majesty.' So one would like to think...

I stop at the grizzled newshormigan's stall on the corner to buy a paper. The Red Sox won't have a snowball's hope in hell of beating the Yankees tonight, he says. I smile and agree.

Go, Yankees! I say. Priding myself on being a master of the forced laugh.

He gives me the thumbs up. I respond in kind. Feigned solidarity! Giving this tweak to my Hormigan-mask, I rejoin the Hormigan rush hour tide.

(I know nothing about the Yankees, and less, if possible, about the Red Sox.)

The Hormigan current draws me into the maw of the subway and down the escalators. A lengthy descent ends finally in the noisy entrails of the city. Barge! Push! Prayers and curses in the Hormigan languages of five continents. Trains come and go unceasingly: Long Island, Queens, Brooklyn Heights, Upper Manhattan, New Jersey. Elbow and shove. Eventually my train arrives. Destination: New Montmartre...

Securing a seat, I ease myself into it and make myself comfortable. I immediately erect a newspaper barrier between me and the Hormigans facing me. The Evil Eye is a much more common phenomenon than is commonly appreciated. That authoritative eye, whose power enters through our eyes, invades the soul and impels our public profession of the Great Hormigan Lie, in all of its obscenity. And so, I shield the windows of the soul behind newspapers, dark glasses, closed eyelids...

The *Megalopolis Daily News* offers me its customary menu: murder, rape, corruption, slaughter, extortion, at national and international levels. Did the eternal sameness of those stories cause me to raise my eyes from the newspaper? Or an idle interest in reading personality from physiognomies? I often kill time on the train between Manhattan and New Montmartre with this guessing game. What thoughts churn behind those impassive foreheads, I ask myself. What fiendish sex acts—or murders—are being imagined, if not plotted, by that Hormigan sitting opposite me as he peruses his copy of *The Weekly World News*?

'*Second World War Aircraft found on Moon*', scream the headlines of that journal. A large black and white apparent photograph of a Grumman F6F Hellcat fighter aircraft resting on a level lunar surface accompanies the report. Proof, if proof were needed, of the total veracity of the story. The off-lead has something to do with Elvis Presley having been photographed, along with Adolf Hitler, in some night-club whose name is obscured by the reader's broad hand.

As I digest these 'facts', I detect a slow footstep on my grave, a strange premonition... but of what? Had some invisible vampire bat from Transylvanian Romania, say, flown suddenly into the carriage? My heart hammers against my ribs as a strange imaginative flip separates me from the other passengers. So that, as they disport themselves on some faraway stage, I gaze down on them from the auditorium balcony.

Has Sonny Boy Death arrived to claim my soul? Without even granting me a glimpse of the answer to life's forever unanswered question? So, there has been an accident and all of us in this carriage are dead? I am surrounded now by corpses? That hellish cacophony—the rhythmic clack or wheel against rail, the tortured squeal of the brakes, an unearthly howl—is an appropriate soundtrack for this grotesque epiphany. Good night Josephine, goodbye Hormiga Tower, Dogfish Head Ale, Zarathustra, Louis Armstrong, intellectual exchanges, Tallisker whisky...

Strange that I hadn't noticed before that young woman sitting just opposite me. She was not there a moment ago. Has that *The Weekly World News* reader just evaporated? I now know for certain that I am dead. And that I now gaze on an otherworldly creature who has taken his place. Her long black hair falls in tresses onto shoulders, smooth as Greek marble. Well-formed breasts, a slender shapely neck, delicately curved eyebrows. No need here to elaborate paeans to perfect feminine beauty, that preserve of romantic fiction writers and *amour courtois* poets. A white dress in contemporary fashion and yet of no age in particular...

Only three stations now, between me and New Montmartre.

Just then I notice three men, conversing with each other in some guttural throaty language I don't recognize. Whose appearance would draw no particular attention in any major 21st century metropolis. They remind me, for no obvious reason, of actors waiting in theatre wings to go onstage. Or how would you, Phantom, explain that adrenaline rush that now traverses my body? Like the sense of excitement a theatre neophyte might feel as the curtain is about to rise on the first act of a drama by Beckett, say. The certainty that I am just about to experience something unusual, unique. And that nothing afterwards will ever be quite the same.

Just then, the knife glitters beneath the carriage lights.

If you crave the sordid details of the 'Knife Incident', sensation seeker that you are, Phantom, I refer you to the *Megalopolis Daily News*, or indeed of any local newspaper. There you will find all the news you seek:

That bone chilling scream still echoes in my brain. The unequal struggle of a woman against three assailants. Help sought in vain from hearts hardened by our Hormigan indifference. A red stain on a snow white dress and then on the floor of the carriage has never stopped spreading.

The *Megalopolis Daily News* shields my eyes from this nightmare. And from that beseeching gaze that accuses. Ensconced in my paper fortress, I read the thoughts of the Hormigan passengers:

—Only fools intervene in another Hormigan's business which, in this case, is rooted, probably, in some murky foreign intrigue. Which has absolutely nothing to do with the solid citizens of Hormiganland?

—What is ordained, is ordained; only fools interrupt the work of the Ladies of the Loom. God alone knows the consequences of facing down those ruffians.

—It would be the height of irresponsibility towards my wife and dependents to involve myself in this fracas.

—Be realistic! What chance would one unarmed citizen have against three murderous assailants? Would his fellow passengers come to his aid? Some hope! For all we know, half of the other passengers are accomplices of the murderers!

My own refusal to act in that Hormigan drama relates to my espousal of the highest value of all: the creation of his own values by this ex-Hormigan who is no longer bound by Hormiga Tower's empty morality.

*What does that mean?*

Look, Phantom! You once held that solidarity based on love of one's neighbor is the highest of all human values. But even you must now realize that such thought is redundant. The supreme value to which I refer is made manifest only among the lofty summits of creativity. The value that distinguishes free beings from those of the Hormigan mob. So, that when Hormigan values conflict with the noble creativity of lonely genius, the highest value must prevail...

That truth being certified by my higher faculties, I now direct my imagination to the well-earned relaxed evening that faces a dedicated post-Hormigan. To those intriguing stories of Umberto Eco that will pair so perfectly with my glass of Highland Malt. The heavenly saxophone of Charlie Parker will drown the sound of this distasteful episode of Hormigan life, the already fading print in tomorrow's *Megalopolis Daily News*. Another cold body on a slab in a mortuary. Another statistic.

Josephine will arrive a little later. Wearing that black dress that so attracts me. To make a few more moves in that chess game we have been playing for some time now. A rapid, self-satisfying coupling, lips on lips, warm body on body...And then away we go to socialize with those artists, journalists and academics who, like us, have abandoned Hormiga Tower to devote themselves single-mindedly to higher things. The sharp witty conversation that is all the more sophisticated for being spiteful, the merciless dissection of some review in the latest *Megalopolis Times* literary supplement.

Oh, how the righteous card-carrying Hormigan would excoriate the callousness of this renegade. And you well know, Phantom, what Hormigans are capable of; the precedents are ominous. They would be sentence me to be hanged, burnt alive, crucified, to death by firing squad

in the name of Hormigan morality

in the name of the Hormigan commandments

in the name of the Hormigan gods...

We reach New Montmartre. Such a ruction! The mob assembles quickly at the station; no novelty compares with the sight of a new corpse. And with the smell of blood. What a story with which to regale unfortunates not present... Police. Security Guards

Reporters. Questions. The same answers I read previously in your minds. With one addendum:

—I slept through the incident! I neither heard nor saw anything.

You can guess my statement to the police!

3.

New Montmartre was enveloped in darkness by the time the police allowed us, the witnesses, to leave the subway station and me to leave that mob of Hormigans behind me.

I pull my coat collar up and set out for my apartment on foot. It is a starry night, a ruddy harvest moon climbs up to the stars. Frost jewels glitter on the sidewalk under the street lights.

I reach the apartment tower at exactly 8p.m. As I ascend to my apartment in the elevator, I fumble in my pockets for the keys. No luck! No sign of them in any of my pockets. Goddam! Not in my briefcase either. Lost or still in the office.

Josephine may have arrived by now. She has her own key. I knock on the door. Silence! Another knock, a little more authoritatively, this time. The same result! No keys! No Josephine within! I put my ear to the door. If Josephine were here she would have heard that knock. And the click-clack of her high heels on the parquet floor inside would resound. But not now.

This is fucking weird! What could be...?

Perhaps Josephine was delayed also!

More work at her office? Her husband may have shown up unexpectedly? That wouldn't be the first time for that irremediable bore to spoil our evening. Josephine left no message in my office. That is most unlike her! But, when I call her number on my mobile, I am informed, coldly, that such a number doesn't exist.

So how do I enter my apartment? Put my shoulder to the

door and knock it off its hinges? This approach, would probably break my shoulder. And, considering door repair costs in Megalopolis, I quickly discount that scenario also.

Nothing to be done, but to return to the street and locate a phone box from which to call Josephine! I'll wait for her in the Scarlet Cockerel on the corner. And meditate over a pint of Samuel Adams on this hyper-complicated day.

I descend once again in the elevator, marveling again at the complete absence of Hormigans in the building. When I reach the front door, I push it open.

## 4.

What awaits me outside freezes the very core of my being.

Has the subzero silence of interstellar space invaded New Montmartre? Unless I am living a ghastly nightmare that hides a more benign reality. All these familiar streets, forever resounding with the roar of traffic, are now completely deserted. Not a single Hormigan, male nor female, not even a dog, on their sidewalks! Nothing moves, excepting the front page of an abandoned newspaper that startles me as it is lifted by a breath of wind, and falls lazily back again.

A panic attack, punctuated by questions, grips me as I struggle to rationalize my situation. Why this apparent absence of life? An unheard air-raid warning? Nonsense! A delayed psychological reaction to that earlier traumatic happening on the train? There are precedents for such...

Or, the question repeats itself, am I myself dead? Of a sudden heart attack on the train? Or was I the victim of those three assailants? Is my isolation that of a corpse? Corpses don't dream! But how do I know that? How can one be certain about anything?

The hollow sound of my footsteps on the sidewalk as I hurry towards the public phone on the corner is anything but ghostly, however. As my mobile is out of action, I can call Josephine from this phone booth. No joy there! I hurriedly phone Hormiga Tower, where there is always an operator on 24-hour duty.

The number you are calling does not exist, says the same staccato female voice.

I then call Police Headquarters. With the same result. And then a series of other numbers that I pick at random from the phone book here in the booth. How can it be that none of these numbers, recorded here in cold print, really exist. Has the emptiness of Hormiga Tower filled New Montmartre? As this hardly deniable truth dawns slowly on me, pure terror is my immediate reaction. If there are no Hormigans to supply food, I tell myself, death from starvation faces me. But, as I find out in the following days, hunger is no problem in the Hormigan-free universe I now inhabit. For, *mirabile dictu*, the shelves of neighborhood stores appear fully stocked every morning. I have no idea from where all that food and drink comes. Nor who supplies it. Nor who consumes it...

As long as the inner man is satisfied, why bother with such questions? Nor ask: from whence come these newspapers on the supermarket shelves with their descriptions of the usual repetitive and predictable events in some imagined Hormigan universe?

Months have passed since the events I described. And— apart from the recorded metallic voice of the telephone lady with whom I commune many times daily—I have yet to see or hear a single Hormigan since the night of the subway train murder. Hormiga Tower is still incommunicado. Completely empty trains communicate between New Montmartre and Manhattan, but I no longer need to work.

What I really miss is the silky softness of Josephine's body as she lay beside me under the sheets. And, with all due respects, your efforts to take her place, Phantom, have had but modest success. However, a person like me must make the best of the strange unsought bargain he has been offered. That, or take leave of his senses.

Ever since I smashed in the door of my apartment with a heavy mallet I found in a nearby hardware store, I spend every day here compiling this diary, when not traversing on foot the squares and parks of the five boroughs of the great deserted city of Megalopolis. The hope, or fear, that I will ever encounter another Hormigan—dead or alive—has long faded. So what!

I believe I have adapted successfully to a new life whose strangeness gets less and less day by day. I now realize that new universes spring from the destruction of the old. True, I shed occasional tears as I remember certain aspects of that old universe of mine. It is not always easy for one who has served an Hormigan apprenticeship to abandon every trace of his conditioning.

*So why don't I stop compiling this diary when there is no being left to read it?*

Excepting you, my dear Phantom, my Bittersweet Consolation!

# BIRTH

**MY BROTHER HENRY AND I** used to share the same bedroom in Glenlongan House. He was, and still is, my junior by a year and a month exactly.

In the night's small hours, the lights of the house having been extinguished and all was in silence, the pair of us would open the blinds and jut our heads into the cool mysterious dark outside. We could hear then the low liquid music of the fountain sounding unceasingly in the center of the neatly trimmed lawn that fronted our not so humble dwelling, referred to as the Big House by the inhabitants of the surrounding countryside. The barking of dogs on distant farms, or of foxes in the surrounding woods, often punctuated those idyllic nocturnal silences.

Ah, those magical nights of my far distant youth, I still imaginatively relive all my sensations of that now distant time as we followed the progress of a full moon bobbing up suddenly from behind the dark woods on the edge of our estate, ascending the starry sky, until it reached the apex of its climb. From there it hung, seemingly suspended on an invisible string from unseen heavenly rafters: a great pale yellow balloon lantern, bathing fields and hedges, the lawn and our stables, in its silver otherworldly light.

As we were chatting quietly and gazing at that moon, Henry swore to me that he could see the features of the man in the moon on that planet's surface. Yes, he said, they are all there. Can't you see them: The nose! The mouth! The eyes! He, of course, could see them all clearly, or so he claimed.

Poppycock, I said to him. You are talking through your hat, Henry. There is no air on the moon for a man to breathe.

Father had let me know that the moon was nothing but a huge rounded sterile rock out there in space, pockmarked with craters, forever circling the earth. Not even a single tree grows on it, he said, not a blade of grass, not a single living thing. It is nothing but a huge naked lump of stone girded by an utter vacuum! Father was chock-a-block with 'nothing buts'. He always had an explanation for every natural phenomenon under the, and beyond, the sun. Said simply, he knew everything.

A few moments later, Henry stretched his forefinger in the direction of the bushes at the bottom of the lawn. I well remember the quake in his voice as he said:

Look! Quickly! I can see some strange thing moving over there by the bushes.

I followed the direction of his finger and, by God, Henry was not joking. Straining my eyes, I could see a dark shapeless form floating silently among the bushes. A cold shiver passed from my head to my toes. Together with all of those other symptoms—pins and needles, hair rising on the back of my neck, etc.—of the terror those macabre stories of Máirtín Rua, Red Martin, always induced in me.

For, according to this *King of the Spalpeens*[11], as we called him, those night hours were the playground of disembodied presences from the other world. And so he introduced us to the

---

[11] *Irish migratory farm laborers.*

*Cóiste Bodhar* (the Silent Coach), the banshee or fairy woman, the *cloorachaun*, the *pooka* and a myriad of other ghostly beings, some of whose ethereal existences depended on blood drunk from the bodies of the living. Just like the horrible wraiths conjured up by the fevered imagination of a Bram Stoker!

To this very day, I can hear the silence he allowed to punctuate his sentences for dramatic effect, so that the horror his words evoked would fully occupy our consciousness and sink into the very marrow of our bones.

That poor unfortunate nun who hanged herself from a branch in the wood over yonder has been seen walking in the fields around here when the moon is full, Máirtín would inform us. Lots of people in the cottages below the fields of the estate have seen her... But not a single person on whom she laid eyes managed to stay alive until the following New Year's Eve. Not a single solitary one! And that is no word of a lie, lads. She scatters death about her as a farmer scatters seed in his fields at springtime.

Both of us fled instantly from the window, just as if God and the devil together had ordered us to do so. Into our beds with us, pulling the bedclothes up over our heads! This was our only defense against the unknown horror lurking outside. Our secret defense works, as it were, within which ghostly presences were invisible to us, and we to them. Or so we earnestly hoped...

When we related the story of the sinister shadow among the bushes to our parents at the breakfast table the following morning, my father gave a loud hearty guffaw:

A ghost, you say? What utter nonsense! There was nothing or nobody outside the house intruding on our property, boys. Absolutely nothing but the creatures of your superheated imaginations! Unless it was Darky or some other dog sniffing around, seeing if they could raise a fox.

He explained to us then and not for the first time, that there was nothing on the surface of this planet but chemicals, whether in living or nonliving matter. And that this was proven beyond any shadow of doubt by the great scientists of England, France and Germany.

And that the imagined beings that people the stories of Máirtín Rua and his ilk were the stuff of superstition, born of ignorance! Old wives' tales whose substance would melt when subjected to the light of pure reason. Naïve imaginings that were forgivable—perhaps—when we consider that their creators had never come into contact with the advanced thought and culture of our epoch! But imaginings that were never to be entertained.

And we, whose highly standing in the Glen had to be lived up to—whose ancestors had, after all, civilized and initiated whatever there is of culture in this stagnant backwater—should pay no attention whatsoever to those outlandish stories. On the contrary:

There is a new era dawning, boys, and people like us have a responsibility to give good example to the Glen people here by rejecting all their medieval obfuscations and welcoming the dawn with open arms. Remember, boys, we are Irish and proud of it.

But not Irish like them!

For, unlike them, our native tongue is English, the language of Swift, Goldsmith and Edgeworth. Our extraction is the extraction of most Englishmen: that is, we have no trace in us out of the aboriginal Irish, the Milesians who came here out of Spain. No, boys, we are genuine typical Irish people of the Danish, Norman, Cromwellian and the Scottish invasions. Our duty is to lead our neighbors, by example, out of the morass of their superstitions to the bright light of reason and rational discourse.

My father reminded me of our local rector, Mr. O'Grady, preaching from the pulpit, when he began to harangue us about our Christian duties in this manner. I am sure that neither Henry nor I understood the half of what he was saying. I think I detected a slight grimace on the face of my mother as Father was holding forth.

After Father had departed for Ballymore—where his court was sitting—she took us aside to explain that total certainty in these matters was never the wisest stance. And that there were certain things, many, many, things in life that had yet to be explained. And that may never be explained...

2.

As far back as I can remember, the spalpeens were a recurrent subject of conversation in Glenlongan House. And for good reason! During the awful years of the Great Famine, which left the West of Ireland decimated, the area that comprises the Glenlongan estate increased appreciably. The majority of the inhabitants of the cottages below our estate were swept towards the famine ships (or towards the graveyard) and their lands thus became available to those who survived that dreadful disaster.

Grandfather acquired the lands he incorporated into the estate at that time by paying for the passage by ship to America of the remaining former tenants of those holdings. As far as they were concerned, it was America or starvation.

This dearth of local inhabitants left him with a labor shortage problem, as it was almost impossible to find a sufficient number of men to carry out the essential tasks that good management of the now enlarged estate demanded. So, when winter turf had to be carried down from the bog, stone walls to be constructed or repaired, seed to be spread in springtime and the harvest to be collected in autumn, and so forth, we depended on spalpeens to ensure that what needed to be done was done.

Henry and I took a keen interest in these spalpeens. They were a very different breed from us. We were told that they came to us from the crags and bogs to the west of Ballymore. And we were given to understand—how I cannot explain—that these wandering farm laborers bore more than their share of original sin. Although we knew quite well that we were far from being perfect—Mr.O'Grady would always be there to remind us of our imperfections in the sight of the Lord—we were, for the most part, clean, responsible, industrious and frugal.

Exactly the opposite of the spalpeens, according to father, or the "aboriginals", as he sometimes called them.

If they were left to their own devices, he said, they would spend their time in drunken revels. Discipline was what they needed! When they were adequately disciplined, it was possible to extract quite an amazing amount of work from them.

The majority of these wandering farm laborers could neither read nor write and few of them were proficient in English. However, they could hardly be blamed for that deficiency. Because, we were told, an understanding of culture or civilized behavior formed no part of their background.

We used to observe them, those *bawneen*[12]-clad groups as they moved along the *boreens*[13] that snake among the rich meadowlands of Glenlongan, the murmur of their Gaelic being carried to us on the wings of the wind. They carried their working tools with them: a scythe slung over the shoulder of one man, another carrying a sickle. For some reason, they reminded us of some broken army, fleeing with their weapons from some dark medieval battle.

Although we and the spalpeens were not of the same blood, we children welcomed their arrival, just as we would welcome the coming of swallows as harbingers of summer. There was an unusual bustle about the place when the spalpeens were in residence, so to speak. We felt somehow that the tyranny of habit had been somehow breached, if only temporarily. For, they would leave us

[12] *white flannel jackets*
[13] *narrow country lanes*

again as soon as the work for which they had been hired by the estate steward was completed. Or, when some strange notion would take them—for the mind of a spalpeen is as difficult to read as the mind of a fox, as my father often said—they would simply take to the road. And the quiet cloak of loneliness would once again fall over the shoulders of the bare hills that surround Glenlongan.

As we grew older, Father impressed upon us continually that the world of the spalpeens and the world of the big house could never be, in any meaningful way, compatible. Our own servants monitored them continually to pick out their faults. A lack of enthusiasm for work in one case. An avaricious look in the eye of another. Or, worse still, the spalpeen who was unwilling to recognize his station in life and who encouraged insolence and disobedience among his fellows.

There was an added need for such vigilance in those days as it was rumored that Fenian organizers, often disguised as spalpeens, were active at the time. My father told us of a wandering American who had sworn hundreds into this nefarious subversive organization in the province of Munster. Luckily for us, our servants were fully trustworthy and supplied us with a running account of all of the doings of the spalpeens who were working for us.

3.

One afternoon, my mother returned from a visit to Ballymore, looking as pleased as a fox that had just spent the night in a hen run. She threw her hat airily from her as she came through the front door. She rapidly ascended the stairs. After adjusting her hair before the big mirror in the upper hallway, and taking a rapid sideways glimpse at that now perceptible swelling of her tummy— which had given Henry and me much cause for speculation—she hurried into the library.

I, being there before her, saw her bestow a rapid loving kiss on my father's forehead, as he raised his eyes, surprised, from the copy of the *London Times* (which was invariably a week out of date by the time it reached Glenlongan) he was lazily perusing. He looked at her inquisitively, his *pince-nez* on the bridge of his nose, as he tried to guess the reason for her good spirits.

Well, what is making you look so happy today, my dear? he said. You seem to be like a cat that has just consumed the most delicious bowl of cream imaginable.

And why not! You know of course that I am just coming from a visit to the doctor?

And what new story has that estimable gentleman to offer us?

Mother was just about to answer this question when she noticed that I was present, my head resting comfortably on the furry stomach of Darky, our household's pet collie. Another stomach that had increased recently in size, by the way!

I still remember that scenario very well. A bundle of comics and adventure stories had arrived from London through the post that morning and lay on the floor beside me. My shoes and socks were covered in mud, as I had spent that rather showery afternoon playing outside. My mother gave a tiny scream before she spoke:

My God! Just look at the cut of you! You look marvelous, or the little I can see of you through the muck that is covering you from head to toe. What in God's name have you been doing to get you into such a state? Even a spalpeen would be ashamed to appear like that.

I let these questions pass over my head, affecting not to hear them as I continued with my reading. Unknown to my mother, I was traveling through the exotic jungles of India at that time, with Kipling's *Gunga Din* as my guide.

Why don't you answer me? Are you deaf, or something, she continued. How dare you drag all that dirt and filth into the house! If

I have told you once, I have told you a hundred times that you are not allowed to go out to play in the mud when it is raining. I do not know what young boys of this generation are thinking half the time. Is it that both of you think you are spalpeens? Sometimes I think that yourself and your brother are living in some dream land!

My mother's protestations just then being to me excessive, if not hysterical, and she seemed to me to be about to break into tears.

Father carefully removed his spectacles and placed them on the mantelpiece just beneath the picture of the Queen. He then laid his newspaper on the small table beside his armchair, put his arm around mother's waist, and drew her towards him. One would think that she resisted this gentle pressure at first. Or at least, she gave the pretense that she was so doing. Until she surrendered and drew in close to him, as both of them spoke in whispers:

Yes, the date has been fixed... and everything is going like clockwork, thank the Lord above!

They continued to murmur on about matters that I was not supposed to understand, according to our Glenlongan House protocol. Those forbidden secrets that pertain to the adult world only. So, I was forgotten temporarily, the warm bulk of Darky as support for my head, as I lay there reading in front of the fire. After a while, realizing that they had no need of my company, I gathered up my reading materials and headed for the Arctic chill of our bedroom.

4.

A short time after that, a new spalpeen came to us looking for work on the estate. He was a well-built young man, although he was only ten years older than me. He had curly red hair that seemed to be a mass of flames, long strong legs, wide shoulders and big hands, with thick veins on the back of them that demonstrated to the world the strength of their owner. His behavior and comportment indicated a self-confident independent spirit, unusual in spalpeens whose humility and fawning ways were a byword among our class. His open face and warm ready smile seemed to indicate that he was of a sunny and honest disposition.

We of the Big House of Glenlongan seldom, if ever, assigned their baptismal names to the spalpeens we had working for us. We had nicknames for them such as The Badger, Snuffles, Wolfhound, Baldy and so forth, based on some outstanding physical characteristic, for those who came to us regularly. His bright red hair could easily have earned him The Fox as nickname, but thanks to our first impressions of him, we departed from our tradition and gave him a human name. For us he was always Máirtín Rua, although we never managed to remember—or ascertain—his surname.

Henry and I were playing in the farmyard the afternoon Máirtín Rua came looking for work, when we were treated then to a sight we could scarcely believe. For there was the same red-haired spalpeen, upside down and walking on his hands along the top of the stable yard wall! His two legs pointing at the sky, as if what he was doing was the most natural thing in the world. That wall was at least ten feet high with an unbroken fall on either side of it. And for pure devilment, and for what he considered to be fun, he whistled a merry tune as he "walked" from one end of the wall to the other, as "surefooted" as a mountain goat walking on level ground.

And then, he launched himself off the top of the wall, performed one somersault in the air before landing on his two feet directly in front of us. He bowed mockingly to us for all the world like one of those acrobats we were taken to see each year at the circus in Ballymore. We had never seen any spalpeen—or anyone else—behave like this before.

When we were in the kitchen later, the serving maids had no other topic of conversation other than Máirtín Rua. These young women were from the cottages below, and strangely enough—

although both cottagers and spalpeens were of the same blood—the former normally took umbrage if they were mentioned in the same breath as the spalpeens. But this spalpeen, Máirtín Rua, appeared to be making an unusual stir among these lassies...

## 5.

We had heard a rumor some time previously that Aunt Amelia in London intended to send us a new brother, or a sister, perhaps. This rumor was now being vigorously recycled. The maids gave us to understand that this living gift was due to reach us any day now. However, I was in some doubt as to this "gift" story, in spite of the sworn affirmations of our informants. My mind had established some connection between it and the swelling of my mother's belly, which could now no longer be concealed.

I was unable to name the basis of my strange suspicion; discussion of such topics was forever taboo in Glenlongan House. What really exercised my imagination, however, was a similar swelling of Darky's belly, although nobody had ever told us that a pup was to be included among the soon-to be-arriving largesse from London. Henry and I discussed these arcane matters but they seemed to be far too complicated for our understanding.

In our bedroom at night, we constantly raked over the uncertainty that attended this mysterious question. One night, as we lay awake into darkness, Henry's whisper broke the silence:

Are you awake, he asked.

Half awake! Why?

No particular reason! But do you know what I heard today?

I have not the slightest idea! That the foxes are taking an interest again in the hen run, or something like that? But tell me what you heard, anyway!

Nothing to do with foxes, anyway. They say that we are going to be sent tomorrow to stay for a week with Miss Willoughby.

We both fell silent. This Miss Gertrude Willoughby, our so-called Aunt Gertrude, was a daughter of Colonel George Willoughby, formerly of the Connaught Rangers, whose fame now mainly derived from his feats of horsemanship with the Galway Blazers Hunt. We knew that he was distantly related to our mother, a consanguinity that caused her to urge us to call his daughter Aunt Gertrude. But, given the cold formality that was part and parcel of the same Gertrude—a rubbing-off on her of the military heritage of her father, perhaps—the condition of "aunt", that I have always associated with sweets and kisses that made me blush, hardly seemed to be appropriate to her.

Gertrude forever felt it her duty to constantly correct our English pronunciation. It had been corrupted, she would say, by the gibberish that is spoken by the cottagers of Glenlongan. If your English sounds like that of those peasants, you will make laughing-stocks of yourselves when your time comes eventually to go to school in England. So, we preferred to call this formidable creature Miss Willoughby, thus denying her the status of aunt-hood, in spite of the imprecations of our mother.

With Miss Willoughby for a whole week! You are pulling my leg. Why would they be sending us to her? Who would ever want to stay again with that awful Miss Speak Correctly the Queen's English? Not to mention that awful lumpy porridge she serves us for breakfast. I hope that you are just having me on!

I wish I was just joking, as you say. But they say also in the kitchen that our new brother will be coming to us from London tomorrow. And, if that is the case, why would they want to send us to Miss Willoughby? Don't think that I want to stay with her any more than you yourself!

We both fell silent. Then I heard Henry sobbing.

What is the matter with you now, Henry?

Nothing!

Then, please be quiet! I am trying to get to sleep...

But Darky is sick, and I heard one of the maids saying that she may die. And mother and Darky are both swelling up in the same way for the last while...

What stuff and nonsense!

## 6.

On the afternoon of the following day our packed bags lay in the hallway with a firm resolve in our young hearts that would not have pleased our parents, had they understood what intention that was exercising our young minds. The horse and carriage that was to carry us the seven miles to the house of the Willoughbys had yet to arrive. As we awaited it, we ate a light meal—cheese sandwiches and milk—in the kitchen. And gooseberry jam made from the produce of the estate. Given that hardly suppressed excitement and conspiratorial whispering of the servants there, it was obvious to us that there was some mysterious business afoot that evening. And to which we scions of Glenlongan House were not to be privy.

But when we heard them say later that the doctor had arrived, we took fright.

Whatever was going on—and it did strike me at the time that it might have had something to do with the present from London—Henry and I were decided that the tyranny of Miss Willoughby was not for us to endure. There was no way we were going to suffer a week-long elocution lesson, no matter what our parents had to say about the matter. If we got the slightest opportunity to slip the leash, then we were resolved that we would seize it.

We had already formulated our strategy. Having escaped from the house, we would hide in a corner of the stables. There, we would be able to carry hay from the loft above and form it into bedding on the stable door, just like the pallets on which the spalpeens slept. We had warm blankets from our own beds, bread, boiled eggs and the other tidbits we had purloined from the kitchen, together with an old oil lamp that was still functioning, all of which were stored in bags that we had waiting for us behind the hedge that bordered the lawn. We had organized everything—all we needed now was an opportunity to escape from the house...

Never in our young lives had we undertaken such an adventure before. Our hearts hammered furiously against our ribs. And our two minds were in turmoil, beset as they were by waves of dread and curiosity regarding the consequences that awaited us if our escape attempt were to fail. Suddenly and unexpectedly, that avidly sought opportunity we so desired presented itself.

Breege, the maid my mother had appointed to take care of us, was told by one of the other maids that her sister wanted to talk to her at the back entrance of the house. Warning us to stay put in the kitchen, she left us to meet her sister. Thus, we were now all alone.

Would we have the courage to seize this opportunity? Would the cowardice that arises from too much contemplation ruin our plan? I looked at Henry and Henry looked at me. I then raised the latch, opened the door and then shut it quietly after us. We then ran like hares across the lawn through the coolness of the dusk until we reached the hedge, gathered the materials that we had stored there and, thus laden, made directly for the stables.

It was early spring nightfall, a yellow frost moon coldly burning there cradled in the nest created for it by the still-naked branches of the trees behind the hedge. There was no sound in the thickening darkness but that unceasing hollow music of water falling into the ornate marble font that encircles the base of our lawn fountain.

We paused and looked back at the house, our ears alert for any sound. Every window in the house was lit up, it seemed.

However, no sound emanated from that direction to indicate that we were the object of some hue and cry. Not yet, at least! But then, when we heard a horse-drawn carriage coming up the driveway to the house, we knew that it was coming to bring us to Miss Willoughby. And that without doubt, within a few minutes, our absence would be discovered.

We were following the line of the hedge until we reached the stable yard, when an unexpected voice in the darkness suddenly raised the hair on the back of our necks.

Hello, lads, and where might ye be going at this time of night?

We recognized the voice of Máirtín Rua. And, as our eyes were becoming more accustomed to the darkness, we saw him standing there beside the door of the first stable. He was not wearing a jacket although there was a hint of frost in the air. But how were we going to answer him? His question challenged us once again from the darkness.

Did you hear me, lads? What are ye doing around here?

Just hanging around, I said. They are busy in the house with visitors...

The red-haired man just laughed when he heard my answer.

"Visitors" is the word all right! The pair of you wandering around out here in the cold and your mother inside popping another one out.

Popping one out? Whatever does that mean?

It was clear from the incredulous grin of the red-haired man—that we could just make out in the weak moonlight—that he could hardly believe that we were unable to understand what he was saying.

You are really not trying to tell me that you don't understand what "popping out" means. Good God above! Do you mean to tell me that you don't know that the baby who was sleeping in your mother's belly, so to speak, has just woken up and is trying to be up and stirring about the place just like myself or yourselves?

This revelation startled both of us. If it was true, why had we been subject to all of this mysterious whispering about a "present from London"? What was the point of such secrecy? I meditated on the words I had just heard for the first time, but I was still unable to imagine the action to which they referred. If the baby was sleeping in my mother's belly, how would it ever be able to make its escape?

I don't know how... I began to say, but I allowed the beginning of my sentence to trail off into silence, leaving it unfinished.

The red haired man was doubled up with laughter.

He seemed to be privy some mysterious understanding that just might be able to blow away that mist of ignorance concerning those secret reproductive matters that our parents had so assiduously conjured up around us. Had this young spalpeen access to the full truth of that mysterious story? Or, more importantly, would he be willing to divulge all, hiding no detail from us, no matter how shameful? These arcane matters were creating a confused din in my head until Máirtín Rua spoke again:

Come along with me, lads! I am going to show you something that I think both of you will be certain to find interesting!

He grabbed our hands and let us into the stable behind him. There was a lantern shining there in the corner. And in the mini-universe defined by the range of its light, what did we see there in front of us but Darky, stretched out on a bed of hay. She didn't jump up to welcome us, as she normally would have done, but lay there weakly, her head resting on her forepaws. She gave us a sorrowful look, her tail managing only the weakest of twitches.

Is Darky dying? asked Henry, with a quavering voice, his mouth encircled by the residue of bread and gooseberry jam.

Dying, you ask? She is far from it; you have not the slightest cause for alarm! Death isn't even relevant here, lads! Because we are talking here about its very opposite, about the appearance of new life itself! You just wait and see!

In spite of this reassurance, Henry remained doubtful. I saw one big shiny tear emerge from his eye, trickle down his cheek and fall off his chin before he asked Máirtín Rua if our own mother was about to die. Once again, a wide delighted grin lit up the spalpeen's features. He impressed upon us yet again that the condition of both Darky and our mother was the very reverse of death, and that both would be as right as rain by the following day.

In the meantime, gather around Darky, boys, for you are about to see something that you have never seen before. Crass ignorance is never to be praised, no matter where it is to be found. It is more than time for young lads like you to grow up fully and understand the living center about which the cycle of life spins.

I will always remember those words of Máirtín Rua and the excitement they created within me. I know that Henry felt the same.

The three of us went down on our knees beside Darky's straw pallet. We focused our attention on two small bundles that reminded us of balls of wool. Each of them was as black as Darky herself, as they lay there beside her teats. The dog wagged her tail weakly again for a few moments. When this wagging stopped, Máirtín Rua instantly bustled into action.

Without drawing a single breath—it seemed—or blinking an eyelid, we watched attentively the approach of Máirtín Rua as he assisted in the birth of the third pup that was emerging from between Darky's hind legs. As he did so, I had an unexpected nervous reaction, such as the spontaneous urge I sometimes have to laugh out loud in church as I listen to the delivery of a solemnly pompous but unintelligible sermon from the mouth of Mr. O'Grady, our pompous but erudite rector. But a long pitiful growl from Darky refocused all my attention to this incredible ceremony that was being directed right in front of us by our pet dog and our red-haired spalpeen.

The appearance of the newborn pup reminded me of a drowned cat I spied once being swept along by the current of the Glen River, each being bathed in some sort of slime. At the same time, there was a smell in the air that reminds me of the smell we were later to experience in the butcher's slaughter house as we gazed—unknown to our elders—on the knifing of sheep. Darky tenderly and carefully licked this small dark bundle she had brought into the world and commenced pushing it gently with her forepaws and nose. But there was no stir whatsoever from the pup. Not even a quiver. It laid there on the straw, a lifeless thing, with no more movement from it than you would expect from a dish rag.

Henry began to sob again, and I must admit that I felt tears well up in my own eyes, though I did manage to manfully keep them back. I was, after all, nine years of age, one year older than him. Máirtín was mumbling a prayer, or something that sounded like a prayer, almost under his breath, his brow puckered with worry. Or so it seemed to me at the time.

Hush, hush, there... There is no need at all to cry... wait until you see... this little pup will live. As sure as eggs are eggs, he will have a long life in front of him. You will see, lads. These words have never failed me. Did he think that the words he was mumbling could somehow stay the advance of death? Father's strictures came suddenly into mind, but the behavior of Máirtín Rua now distracted me from them.

For, he started to pull gently on the pup's legs, pushing and massaging slowly and rhythmically the tiny inert body of the pup with his long strong dirty fingers. He continued doing so without any obvious result. Forever, it seemed to me. The beads of sweat on his forehead glistened in the weak light from the lantern as he repeated under his breath this prayer—if, indeed, prayer it was—time after time. Meanwhile, his eyes stared, expressing the full desire of his soul and body, as it were, to will life into the motionless body of the pup. It seemed to me that the whole universe had shrunk to the two hands of our spalpeen pushing and kneading without cease.

Suddenly the miracle happened. Life exploded in that inert mass of flesh under the unceasingly moving fingers of Máirtín Rua. The first twitch of the pup's body startled me like a sudden electric shock. And then another twitch, followed by a cascade of twitches! But our spalpeen continued to knead the pup until the full rhythm of life was beating, strongly and regularly, in that small body. Only then did he place the pup gently down beside Darky's teats. There it is, boys; the job is done! Remember that I told you that there was never the slightest cause for anxiety!

But it seemed to us that Máirtín, just like us, was invaded by a deep sense of relief. And when that friendly grin spread across his face, we also felt the tension draining out of us. He picked up a large dirty handkerchief—"rag" would be a more appropriate word—from the floor beside him and started to rub his face and his hands with it.

Well, boys, was that your first time seeing this sort of work?

I felt that I had just had an opportunity now to get a definitive answer to a certain question that had been exercising my curiosity for some months now. And that it would have been improper of me to seek that answer from my parents in that Big House across the way. They would have been shocked at my effrontery, I am sure, in broaching a matter that should have been anathema for one of my tender years. Asking the serving maids was out of the question.

But now I summoned up my courage and put the question directly, if somewhat shamefacedly, to Máirtín Rua. He answered me directly and simply in the language of the cottages and of the crags and bogs to the west of Ballymore. An answer that would have been unacceptably obscene, of course, had it been expressed in the language of Glenlongan House! But that was natural and innocent, without any hint of indecency, as it rolled musically off the tongue of Máirtín Rua in his native language.

It seemed to me somehow that night that I had begun to leave the blinkered existence of a child behind me and that I had taken one faltering step, however tiny, into the mysterious world of adulthood.

Later that evening, when our "naughtiness" had been forgiven us, effaced quickly by the excitement that surrounded the "gift"—named Sophie— that had come to us from London, remember, we were conducted into our parent's bedroom that we might see mother and the recent arrival. She was sitting up in the bed, smiling, as she looked down lovingly on the "gift"—a tiny doll-like pink creature wrapped in a white shawl—lying and screaming on the bed beside her.

Take a look at your new sister, boys, she said. She is the present I was telling you about that your aunt was going to send us from London. Well, here she is, at last! Isn't she just a darling? I said nothing but Henry piped up:

A present? Was she really sent from London?

My brother was just about to give the game away. I figured that he was just on the point of refuting mother's white lie with the truth, as we had learned it from the lips of Máirtín Rua over in the stables. I could not allow him to spill the beans. So, when he felt the dig of my elbow in his ribs, he got the message and clammed up.

It would have been neither worthwhile nor advisable to deny the veracity of mother's claim.

Wasn't it enough that we had observed with our own eyes the mystery of birth, beside whose profundity those ridiculous stories we had been fed us to cloak nature's raw reality paled into utter insignificance. With the wisdom of hindsight, I am sure that just at that point a breach opened between myself and the world of my parents and started to widen.

But if either my father or my mother knew that the mystery of both human and animal reproduction was no longer a secret for their sons, thanks to Máirtín Rua's intervention, the latter's stay with us would be instantly terminated.

## 7.

Máirtín Rua kept on coming to us year after year. And as far as we in Glenlongan House were concerned—and especially Henry and I—he was always our King of the Spalpeens! Almost everyone loved and respected him. And, hadn't we boys seen those big strong hands of his coax life from death?

I know very well what my father would have had to say about those unintelligible mysterious incantations, if such they were, the red-haired man gave voice to in order to raise that pup from certain death. Superstitious gobbledygook, or something of the sort! However, be that as it may...

The servants, along with us, were enchanted by the stories of Máirtín Rua. His words transported us thousands of miles away from the gray daily reality of Glenlongan to visit magical lands that the London magazines, as good as they were, never managed to reach.

His storytelling prowess was no hindrance whatsoever to his being simply the best workman to ever undertake the multitudinous tasks our estate needed to be performed to ensure its continuing viability. It seemed to us that there was no task, however complicated, with which our red-haired spalpeen could not be entrusted. As a handyman he had no equal. Masonry or carpentry, they were both grist to his mill. Working mainly by himself, he managed to build our new stable. And, miraculously, he was able to repair permanently the kitchen clock that had been to-ing and fro-ing for years between Glenlongan House and a Dublin clock repairer. There seemed to be no end to the talents of this Jack of all trades from the mysterious territory to the west of Ballymore.

Although it may be difficult for some to believe, as I recall the minutiae of those golden days, we had absolutely no idea as to how or where Máirtín Rua lived outside the periods he spent with us in Glenlongan. Nor could we say from whom he traced his descent nor what sort of education, in the widest possible sense of that word, he had received before the sojourns he spent with us. Or what he would do, or how he would spend his time, in those intervals when he was not employed by us.

We questioned him regarding these matters now and then.

But Máirtín himself forever enjoyed blunting the edge of our curiosity with a joke or some amusing story that made us forget our question. In the end, Henry and I desisted from posing such. Quite simply, we were unable to imagine that Máirtín Rua had an independent life outside the small cozy universe of Glenlongan.

Or, what amounts to the same thing, his life—as far as we were concerned—took up where it had left off as soon as he appeared at our door after having spent some time away from us, Darky, happily barking her welcome for him! But his life became a *terra incognita* once again when the harvest was in and stored and as soon as his broad back disappeared from view at the bottom of the avenue to our house.

Máirtín Rua's English has really improved. I would really like to do something to improve his lot in life. Or so my mother said a number of times. As Henry and I were now teenagers—and at school in England for much of the time—and Sophie was an independent-minded young girl determined to cast off clinging maternal ties, mother was now devoting much more time to charitable work.

My father donated his cast-off clothes, which were still like new, except to the over-perceptive, and eminently wearable—suits, shoes, shirts and so forth—to Máirtín. And when our favorite spalpeen was togged out in this finery, no one would ever have believed that he was really a spalpeen. Rather, he appeared more like one of our gallant young country gentlemen. Indeed, until he opened his mouth to speak, he was sometimes taken for a visiting relative of our Glenlongan House family.

It was common knowledge among the kitchen staff, as might be imagined, that more than one young woman in Glenlongan was head over heels in love with our Máirtín. And that all he would have to do was pop the question, and he could have as his bride the pick of the valley's beauties. And I know now, from reading my father's diaries and the estate records, that Máirtín was offered the position of steward of our estate, with the responsibility of overseeing all agricultural activity there. No other person of the spalpeen breed had ever been promoted to such an elevated position. What a fine catch he would have made then for some ambitious young maiden!

8.

But for reasons that we didn't understand at the time, and still don't understand, Máirtín elected to turn down this generous offer. And, then, he suddenly refused to wear my father's cast-off clothes. And, whatever madness possessed him, he started to wear again those symbols of spalpeen poverty: grubby homespun tweeds and those torn *bawneen* cardigans that nobody to the east of Ballymore would ever be caught dead wearing. When, one day, my father summoned Máirtín to his study and questioned him about the new regressive direction his life appeared to be taking, he received the following apocryphal answer:

*Arrah*, however could a man of the Big House ever understand the mind of a spalpeen!

Father recalled that Máirtín's features clouded over as he, Father, was trying to make sense of what he had just said. He concluded that such a form of words served merely to divert his attention from whatever was really at the bottom of our recidivist spalpeen's mind. Or perhaps Máirtín himself did not really understand the sense of the *shibboleth*[14] he had just mouthed.

And what sort of unintelligible and ungrateful answer is that coming, as it does, coming from someone we had always treated with affection and generosity and who, by this time, has almost become a member of our household?

Máirtín shrugged his shoulders and didn't add to his answer to Father's question. A few minutes later, outside the house, the old familiar Máirtín reappeared. He whistled a merry tune and an urge for devilment once again manifested itself in those deep blue eyes of his.

At about that time, however, Máirtín began to absent himself without explanation from the estate. At first, we hardly noticed this new tendency. He would be gone for short intervals, a fortnight or three weeks at the most. The first time this happened, he returned somewhat shamefacedly, informing my father that he had been feeling ill. Father immediately called Dr. O'Brien, our local doctor.

The latter, after examining Máirtín, pronounced him to be as fit as a fiddle. But we noted, with dismay, that these absences occurred more frequently now and were becoming increasingly longer. The excuses with which he tried to explain these derelictions of duty were becoming less and less credible. In fact, his behavior was becoming so unpredictable and his answers so erratic that father realized that questioning him about his absences was a total

---

[14] *truism*

waste of time.

To make matters worse, the easy relationship that Henry and I used to enjoy with Máirtín underwent a change for the worst as we advanced into our teens. Instead of being greeted with the old familiar "lads", we had now graduated to being addressed as "sir", expressed with an obvious undercurrent of cynicism. Almost as if our erstwhile hero was trying, consciously, to widen the breach between us and the secret life he hid from us and to which he seemed to be inexorably drawn.

Where did Máirtín stay when he was not sleeping in Glenlongan? In Ballymore? Or further to the west in his native haunts? Who knows! In any case, my parents were very worried about the effect of his absences.  For, Máirtín's wanderings demonstrated clearly to them just how basic his work output was to the ordered functioning of the estate. One man who can do, and does, the work of two, or even three, is hardly ever dispensable in such a context.

Father tried to get to the bottom of the story, one fiercely rainy afternoon when all work outside had been suspended while the rain lasted. But after he and Máirtín had spent more than an hour talking to each other in the library, the curt nod father gave to us on emerging from this conclave indicated the hopelessness of the case. Absolutely  no solution after all that palaver! Henceforth, we would have to suffer the surliness and inefficiency of workers who came to take Máirtín's place.

### 9.

One fine sunny day, our red-haired spalpeen departed from us and we were not to have any sight or news of him for a very long time afterwards. However, we did manage eventually to get some tidings of him. One gloomy wet and windy afternoon, father came back from court in an obvious bad humor. It seems he managed to locate Máirtín and that our old friend was in the poorest shape imaginable. And residing in the Poor House, of all places! And before that he had lost his right foot in an accident on the Ballymore docks. This news horrified us. And even worse, father said that Máirtín's health had been seriously undermined by months of heavy drinking.

That damned poteen has wrecked his constitution, he said.

Máirtín Rua a drunkard! Who would ever believe such a thing was possible? And what a sad explanation that was of the months he had spent wandering after he left our Glenlongan! Now we understood, ruefully, the fate of the clothes my father had so generously presented him. It seems that he sold them all in order to acquire the wherewithal to support his drinking habits. And once he had enough money saved, he would disappear from view again, without any of us ever suspecting the dark secret that was destroying him.

In spite of all this negativity, I still had a yearning to encounter the hero of my boyhood once again. And with that intention in mind, I made for the Poor House in Ballymore one winter afternoon. And it was there I came upon Máirtín Rua, sitting on the ground with his back to the wall among some other equally disheveled wretches. A wooden crutch lay on the ground beside him. His blue eyes lit up with a glimmer of recognition when he saw my eyes seeking him out. He tried to stand up. But when I noticed how difficult that was for him, I asked him to stay sitting.

You are welcome here, sir, he said, with a rasping hoarse voice.

I reached out towards him and we shook hands. But that glimmer in his eyes slowly faded and died as I rabbited on about world affairs, about the Boers, the campaigns in Africa and the successes our forces were enjoying there, about how lonely we felt for Glenlongan and Ireland when we were at school in England, about the rumor that the Fenians were active and drilling in

Glenlongan, about the petty affairs of the Big House, about the appointment of Henry as captain of the school rugby team, about the weather, even...

But, to make a long story short, it seemed clear from the outset that we had nothing to say to each other. I even mentioned that event in the stables, a long time ago, when his hands had managed to snatch a young pup from the jaws of death. But his eyes were empty as he looked at me, giving me to understand that he had not the slightest idea of what I was talking about. And that he and I no longer inhabited the same world.

As I looked there, in the Poor House, at that swollen face with its network of broken veins and at those bleary eyes in which all hope and happiness appeared to be extinguished, how could I relate them to the image I have of a younger energetic Máirtín Rua, upside down and walking on his hands along the top of the stable yard wall of Glenlongan House. For this Máirtín sitting right in front of me seems to be drained of all energy, with those great hands of his that once snatched life from death one magical evening now lying idly there on his lap. Can it really be that this listless malodorous old man, dribbling there in front of me, is only ten years older than me?

I felt embarrassed and out of place standing beside him, my erstwhile hero, recognizing that my stories and rumors from Glenlongan were just so much chaff, petty gossip, beside a personal disaster I could not explain, embodied here in front of me in the empty shell of the Máirtín Rua who had once opened for me the gates of adulthood...

What dreadful abyss lay under the life of the spalpeens that one of the best of their kind could fall into such a lamentable state, rejecting the help that we were always more than willing to give him at any time? Having muttered my excuse—a nonexistent appointment in the town for which I was already late—I took my leave of him. I am sure he didn't note my departure with those deep blue eyes of his that now seemed to be permanently fixed on a landscape that I would never see.

The story of Máirtín's accident, and the state in which it had left him, convulsed the entire household. Corporal works of mercy were my mother's automatic reflex by this time to stories of such appalling misfortune, and she sent another supply of father's cast-off garments to him, accordingly. With the power and influence he had as Her Majesty's magistrate in Ballymore, my father was able to ensure that our red-haired acquaintance would receive preferential treatment at the Poor House. And when he promised my father that he would return to Glenlongan, my mother organized a money collection from the houses of the neighborhood in which Máirtín had sometimes worked. With the proceeds of this collection she was able to buy for him an artificial leg of the latest design.

But, despite of this effort and the spalpeen's promise to my father, we were destined to see neither this artificial limb nor its would-be owner, Máirtín Rua, ever again.

10.

The days of our youth in Glenlongan are recalled sometimes—and somewhat emotionally—by Henry and I when we meet and talk over port in our club in London.

It is some time now since we discussed Máirtín Rua, however. Although I find it impossible to understand, my brother claims that he has no memory whatsoever of that personage. No account I give of the deeds of Máirtín, and the way they impinged on both of our lives, finds not the slightest resonance with Henry. He suggests that they must be descriptions of the deeds of some wildly improbable character I have been encountering in a dream or in a book. So he mocks me, in a joking brotherly way, any time I mention this King of the Spalpeens. I tell him that his brain must have been curried by the Indian sun, or addled by Imperial port, and we both burst out laughing.

And then again, I remind myself that my brother is an extremely busy man these days, with no time for nostalgia or fantasy. He was always ambitious, taking after father in that respect. And ever since his return from his apprenticeship with the Indian Civil Service, his rise in the ranks of the civil service here has been meteoric. Therefore I am disposed to accept the idea that his memories of minor personal details, without much relevance to his career, as far as he is concerned, have been consigned by him to oblivion.

As far as I am concerned, however, I have to admit that I am not very practical person. Both Henry and Sophie insist that I am givento dreams and romanticism. I do not subscribe at all to their judgment. My rational self is passionately involved in entomological research, for example. And a book I have just written concerning my findings in regard to the reproductive processes of ants—based on the studies I have conducted throughout the Empire—is shortly to be launched by one of our more prestigious scientific publishers here in London. I like to think—in fact I am certain—that my lifelong fascination with the processes of nature is a part of the heritage that Máirtín Rua bequeathed to me.

Having said that, and arising from my conversations with Henry and Sophie, I have noticed for some time that the house of my boyhood in Glenlongan, and all of the memories that go along with it, are becoming hazily dreamlike in my mind. At least Henry's account of Foreign Office infighting and Sophie's hobnobbing with suffragettes and London's Irish literary set, Yeats and Shaw and their ilk, have verifiable referents. But I mention specific events of our shared history—Darky's parturition, above all—and the two of them look at each other, their eyes asking silently: whatever in God's name is he talking about?

To the extent that their doubt has now transmuted into my self-doubt! So that I torture myself by asking: did that Máirtín Rua really exist? Or was he a ghost? Or some creature of my own imagination summoned up by it to answer to some mysterious need of mine that I cannot understand? What I can say with certainty is that my memory—or this strange repetitive dream—focuses on the clear image of the strong rough fingers of Máirtín, as they coax new life out of inert clay. But are those fingers any more real than those phantoms, as he described them in their most lurid detail that chilled us to the marrow, seemingly aeons ago, in the kitchen of Glenlongan House?

Or are they more real than the bright moon suspended there over dark hedgerows in the silence of those far-off Glenlongan nights?

Perhaps, all of these were dreams as well.

# BLEEP

**GREAT TO HEAR FROM YOU,** old pal!

And many thanks for giving me a shout! As it happens neither me nor Soraya, nor the cat are in right now—if indeed we were ever "in" in the precise sense that you probably mean that word—but if you would be so good as to leave your name and number, I will call you back later. This I solemnly promise; I cannot, of course speak on behalf of the cat, and as for Soraya... Just speak after the bleep...

Don't call me "pal"! I'm no 'pal' of yours, nor would I want to be counted among your friends. I don't even recognize your voice. What or who in the hell might you be? Is this some sort of an adolescent joke, or what?

Or maybe just another technical fault, old pal! You hadn't considered that, had you? The aforementioned bleep may be subject to a slight delay, sir. So while we are waiting for that magical electronic ping, I strongly advise you to listen very carefully to what I am about to tell you. For, let me solemnly promise you, the commentary you are about to hear to is going to turn that grey comfort zone in which you live—through no fault of your own, by the way—upside down, inside out, *topsy turvy*, or however you like to phrase it. In the process, though, some basic truths will become manifest, shot through with those inevitable glimpses, alas, of the bestial floor. In any case, no more hubristic outbursts, if you please!

As if a rare star, whose existence you never even suspected, swam suddenly into your ken. I can appreciate that this unexpected and exclusive offer, made on a rainy night such as this, may come somewhat as a shock to you. For who would ever suspect a mere voice mail, to which I am reduced at present, to be capable of such a *spiel*. Explanations will follow in due course. *Honest injun*! In the meantime, I digress; garrulity is my stock in trade, if not my passion...

Nevertheless, a cautionary word before I move on from this stepping stone: don't assume for a split nanosecond that this humble word-smith, whose voice is beamed directly at you from this voice mail, is a right-thinking, courteous, well-mannered hail-fellow-well-met human being. Indeed, those in the know would argue, correctly, that the use of the word "human" is away more than excessive as applied to my case. Be that as it may, let me make it clear, abundantly clear, that I hope that all is well with you and yours on this glorious starry night, that your dog sleeps soundly on his accustomed full stomach of canned old donkey and that your cat has been put out to earn her keep a' hunting rodents until the dawn pales the eastern reaches of a night sky enlivened by star blink.

Aha! I can detect now one of the many questions that are bouncing around in your brain. Namely: am I really listening to the voice mail of a friend who has temporarily, and with no malice aforethought, absented herself from her lawful abode? Or that of a pseudo friend who, knowing that it is you calling her, willfully and with malice aforethought decides to bamboozle you with empty verbiage?

Now, here is another consideration! Has it occurred to you, that this stream of words entering your warm inquisitive ear, pressed as it is to the receiver, issues from no living throat? Even that you may be listening to a disembodied voice, untrammeled by that loathsome space-time horizon that so imprisons your own poor human flesh. For, unlikely as it may seem to you, the voice you are hearing is time-old, although in the context of the limitless reality I inhabit, time itself is an empty concept. This is the very context which I would like you to imagine, if you can. Weird? But fear not; I can understand you. "Time" and "journey" are metaphors that have, for me, an occasional utilitarian value.

Sorry! Your poor addled earthling brain is confused by my polysyllabic chat and I detect that you are about to give vent to some sarcasm before you hang up on me! Am I older than the *Hag of Beare*[15]? I hear your question before you are able to articulate it! But, I warn you, speak not until you hear the bleep. Otherwise, the Fates will intervene, and not so peacefully, say I, being gifted with foresight as well as hindsight.. You have been warned. The *Hag of Beare*, indeed! She has yet to become a glint in her father's eye in the universe I inhabit as well being reduced to a handful of dust scattered among the stars. What sort of a lunatic are you dealing with? You ask silently. Of course I can read your mind, silly boy. But when I tell you that this unidirectional communication has its origins in *Log na nDeamhan*[16] I know that you think I have gone teetotally gaga.

Oh, I am fully aware that you are asking yourself: where in the name of almighty fuck is this Hollow of the Demons? But will you please shut up until I have finished what I am saying. I haven't interrupted your stream of consciousness; don't interrupt mine until you hear the bleep.

Now let me say that I do welcome your question and I do fully support your democratic right to ask it. Indeed I regard it not only as your right but as your democratic duty to interrogate everything and anything. It is a principle that I would hold myself,

---

[15] *An ancient poetic symbol of Ireland.*
[16] *Hollow of the Demons*

were I wearing human shoes, and I know that many of you out there are troubled by the current democratic deficit in advanced technological societies. Indeed, I would be so troubled by this question, were I a member of your race, that I would, unhesitatingly, go so far as to establish an interparty subcommittee whose remit would be to come back to us, after a period appropriate to their deliberations, with practical proposals that would leave the exchequer totally unscathed.

What in the hell are you talking about?

Sorry about that, but—as can, and does, happen to bishops—my thought got on a track of total irrelevancy and wound up spouting pious nonsense that has nothing to do with so-called 'real life'. So, where were we?

Ah, yes! At the Hollow of the Demons. That is where we were. Let's have a toast, then! A health to all in Ireland, and in the County of Mayo, and the creep who doesn't like us, may he rot in hell below! For that is where the aforesaid Hollow is located, my friend: in the fair County of Mayo. It is necessary to state this at the outset, because you and I both know that the generation that now treads old Erin's rain cursed meadows is blind—as blind as poor fuckin' Balor after they poked his one eye out—to the facts of its own history and geography. [17]

There is history and history, of course. And I am afraid that you know nothing of the chapter I am about to relate to you. But you need to know it if you are ever to make sense of this little drama in which you are an unwitting participant. In which you are, believe it or not, about to make a guest appearance in the leading role. After the bleep, of course.

Please don't even consider hanging up on me at this point. This story isn't altogether bad and I can promise you that it gets better and better, even if I say so myself. Just keep on reminding

---

[17]  *A one-eyed demonic figure in Irish mythology.*

yourself that you are already acting in this drama. Even if you are not aware that you are! Yes, my friend, there you are, already on the stage, in the starring role, and giving the thespian performance of the century...

So where does this Hollow of the Demons come in? It is a long and mournful story!

Long, long ago—and as long as long can be—Saint Patrick was fasting and praying, as was his wont, on the top of the mountain now known as *Croagh Patrick*, in the fair County of Mayo. His craw thumping and great pious sighs greatly discommoded our company who had been residing on that same mountain for aeons previous to his arrival. And whose intention was to reside there for aeons after his departure. We were a merry company then, and still are, all things considered. As you will find out for yourself long before that fateful bleep puts an end to this pleasant one-way communication!

Never, but never, mess with us! You have been warned.

In any case, there were those in our midst who grew tired, to phrase it as delicately as I can, of the unending stream of Latin invocations carried by the wind to our ears (I speak metaphorically) at the most inappropriate hours from the mouth of that foreign proselytizer. The barbarous sound of his demotic British Latin was an especial irritant, misshapen as it was by the pronunciation of his native Strathclyde Welsh, to those of us who had come to appreciate the virtues of correctly pronounced literary Latin. Therefore, I stress, the sentiment that impelled many of us to seek the expulsion of this obnoxious foreign witch-doctor from our mountain was far from being racist. Esthetic reasons, almost exclusively, fuelled our attempts to rid ourselves of such an unwelcome noisemaker.

I would like to stress here also that we were a liberal, tolerant, community in those good old days. At the same time, we clearly understand the clear logical implications of that ancient saw: to every cow its calf. *Mutatis mutandis:* to every habitat its inhabitants *recte:* its original inhabitants. So that this Patrick (along with every Christ-crazed interloper, every bloody one of them, who dragged their miserable leather skinned *currachs*[18] up the beaches of old Erin of the *crannógs*[19]) should betake himself back rapidly to whatever cesspit from which he had crawled in the first place. And to desist forthwith from his attempts to subject the valiant merry race of Ír and Éibhir to the powers of his crosier. Not to mention the zeal with which these loons filled their gluttonous stomachs with such rich wild boar cutlets and venison steaks as the vast woodlands of the aforesaid territory amply provided.

Although we gave him fair and appropriate warning, written neatly in Latin upper case script on the wings of the wind, Patrick gave us no sign whatsoever that he was about to move his blessed ass elsewhere. And, as we were —and are— nothing but disembodied speech, we lacked the feet, bone and muscle needed to propel with well-directed kicks that god-struck loon from our midst. Things rested so, until our own dear mother, the oft-belching sweet-farting Caorthannach—that powerful shrewd woman— arrived on the battlefield.

Blows reach the bone, she announced in thunderous tones, but words are swept away by the wind, a state of affairs of which our kind is painfully aware. Thus, somewhat anomalously, that famous word-battle between our Caorthannach and that sour Christian crank commenced. Sound raged against sound. Wise words were overcome by wiser yet words. One unaccountable byproduct of this summit meeting was a transubstantiation achieved by our Caorthannach who, by dint of wizardry, converted

---

[18] *A type of Irish boat with a wooden frame, over which animal skins or hides were once stretched.*

[19] *A partially or entirely artificial island, usually built in lakes, rivers and estuarine waters of Scotland and Ireland.*

our essential nothingness into flesh. And, incredibly, all of us were incarnated there as ravens, ready to pit beak and claw against that mean-spirited craw-thumper who laid claim to the peak of our mountain.

We went on the attack bravely and boldly. Our wings, beating in fury, darkened the skies over our holy mountain and over the shiny bald pate of that foreign bearded God-prattler.

I hope that you are listening carefully to all that I am saying and taking in the details of my story as you wait there for that bleep.

The spouter of bog Latin called upon his Lord God to rout us. But that eminence was, apparently, attending to some urgent business or other on the other side of the Milky Way at that time.

So that this Welsh thug, Patrick, spawned in the cesspits of Strathclyde, was obliged to have recourse to that magic bell that was never far from his side. The magic of this bell was stronger than the most powerful spells we could muster, according to the usual reliable sources we consulted. Patrick was now waving it, menacingly, at us. I must admit that this maneuver frightened us. An unverified rumor, then doing the rounds, held that the same bell had caused a sow to give birth over to the East, in the Laighnibh country, a few weeks previously to a piglet with a seal's head. True or untrue? One never can tell!

To be on the safe side, however, and complying with the principle that states that a good retreat is better than a bad stand, we got the hell out of there as fast as we could. This disorderly rout—the naked, albeit bitter, truth may as well be admitted here—continued until we reached the Hollow of the Demons, at some remove from the summit of our beloved mountain.

Worse was to follow. Can you believe that Patrick was so incensed, or frightened, that he hurled his accursed bell after us? The unmerciful clang that it made as that fuckin thing smashed against a granite boulder set terrified wild deer a running *helter skelter* through the woods of the five provinces of old Erin. The noise gave us such a start that we left our raven bodies there behind us in the lonely Hollow of the Demons. So that we became unfleshed words once again, condemned to wander forever in this, the weirdest dimension of all in our infinitely dimensioned universe.

I am aware that folkloric accounts hold that Patrick then threw the bodies of the ravens—or of the demons that we are frequently alleged to be—into the Atlantic Ocean between the islands of Acaill and Cliara.

And that was meant to be that! So from incomplete accounts of this unhappy event, as viewed through uni-dimensional human eyes, grew the egregiously false myth that the now sainted Patrick Calpurnius expelled for ever all demons and serpents from the soil of Ireland. Those of your fellow countrymen who choose to lend credence to this grossly distorted version of the facts, as they unfolded, on that fateful day on Croagh Patrick fish for definitive meaning in the murky waters of non-reality. Things are seldom (possibly "never") what they seem to humankind.

Am I boring you? If so, you are probably laboring under the misapprehension that this narrative is of no concern to you. How totally wrong you are! For, believe me, your very fate is integral to this very narrative. I can read the thoughts that are racing through your mind as I speak but, believe me again, to hang up on me now would be the most ill-considered step you ever have taken. Among the other misfortunes that would befall you if you take that step, you would lose that magnificent life-changing prize that I am keeping here especially for you.

Think about it!

And wait for the bleep before you open your mouth. Patience is the virtue you must cultivate. Always! This is my advice to you—and I have my reasons—although you may consider that the folkloric ramblings of a voice mail are a pure waste of time. If this is your stance, what would you say if I told you that you are listening right now to one of those aforementioned disembodied voices? *Shhh*! Please keep your gob shut until you hear the bleep!

For I am but one disembodied voice trapped in one strange universe in the infinity of parallel universes that constitutes the very ground of reality! Let us leave aside the physical, metaphysical not to say ontological dimensions of the problem of reality to address ourselves to the practical difficulties encountered by a flock of disembodied words such as we are which has wandered the highways and bye-ways of Ireland ever since the cruelest of fates befell us in that thrice accursed Hollow of the Demons.

Our *hegira* was not without its amusing moments in the old days. Consider the fears that beset your ancestors when we manifested ourselves to them through a variety of forms, such as: the *Púca Mór* (the Great Pooka), the *Cóiste Bodhar* (The Silent Coach), the *Colainn gan Cheann* (the Headless Corpse), the *Cailleach gan Chíocha* (the Breastless Biddy), the *Bean Sí* (the Fairy Woman) the *Bóbodha Gharraí na bhFataí* (the Potato Garden Ghost), the *Bodach gan Bhod* (the Dickless Dastard), even *Learaí an Leipreachán* (Larry the Leprechaun) or the *Cluaracháinín na gCluas Ceathartha* (the little pointy-eared *Cloorachaun*).

Consider the heat that was generated, as we listened to your ancestors as arguing our very existence with great mountain-shaking Gaelic oaths and raucous table-banging until the blinding lights supplied by the Electricity Supply Board drove us eventually from this vale of tears into the outer darkness.

Or so it seemed!

I'll bet it never occurred to you that ingenious folk like us, survivors of the Hollow of the Demons fiasco, who were there for an infinity of aeons before the Big Bang instituted your meaningless universe (and who will be there as your beloved solar system is sucked in to your dying sun) could find a method to overcome our condition. Nor that we would be sufficiently able and knowledgeable to easily master the crude intricacies of contemporary technology. Thus, we were able, with contemptible ease, to colonize quietly the very "cutting edge" instruments of communication technology in spite of the security mechanisms put in place by that simpleminded Johnny-come-lately, the human being.

None of this occurred to you, of course.

Hard to blame you, though!

Who would ever imagine folk as ancient as us—*Tuatha Dé Danann*, fairy folk who predate time, denizens of the fairy forts of the Irish countryside, whose essence cannot even boast form, who predate the human race, and the Planet Earth itself, to have such sophisticated capabilities. And then you may ask yourself: if we are preverbal beings, free from the vagaries of the flesh, then your earthling logic dictates that we have no yardstick with which to measure truth and falsehood. And that every statement we emit, by whatever means, is an empty hypothesis that is never amenable to proof or falsification. .

It seems to me that you have lost the thread of my argument—as, indeed, as I have myself—as some *non sequitur* seems to have intervened somewhere along the line. Who cares! For whirl is king, the only king, in the dark realm we inhabit. My apologies for plying you with all of that abstract stuff, my friend. A little bit of philosophical speculation now and then passes the time agreeably. A harmless pastime, let us say, as long as you never take its conclusions too seriously! But as we are abstract beings ourselves, just as the otter is attracted to water, and dung-beetles to cow-pats, we are sometimes enthralled by the abstraction that is native to us...

But enough of that! Let me put some new twist in this monologue to pass the time until... Ooops! I was just about to say it.

Just caught it in time! Forgive me my indiscretion! I almost reached the end of the story, omitting all the juicy intermediate bits....

Concentrate immediately, if you will, on the strategic advantages conferred on us by our new electronic home. Looking back on the long doleful history of the wandering of our race on this planet, through folklore after folklore, it would occur to the informed observer that Nikola Tesla, the Serbian electrical genius, was the human catalyst who guided us into our promised land. For, it is a fact that there was no comfort at all to be had in those damp fairy forts that dot the Irish landscape. I think of those crowded quarters, those perpetually leaking roofs, those sullen turf fires, with a shudder.

Compared to such discomforts, the silicon chips we now inhabit are both dry and clean. And that isn't all. Get your head around the fact that every single communication that moves telephonically, for example, is scrutinized by us. Whether we are talking of gentle soothing words between lovers, e-mails, hot money on its way to the Cayman Islands, radio programs, messages between governments or government departments —it is all the same to us. So you cannot fool us; we have learned all the languages; we know all that is going on.

There is more. We the bodiless survivors of Calpurnius' ire at the Hollow of the Demons enjoy a mischievous sense of humor. The lore of the common folk incorporated that verity, at least. If we have such unlimited powers, why not enjoy them. But we are of a hell a long way from such old-fashioned stuff as souring milk and neutralizing the fertility of cattle, let me assure you, dear friend. Now we can play with mankind's messages, changing a word here and a word there to completely alter the sense of electronic communications.

For example, we love to change key words in carefully worded messages between governments in consonance with our wicked (as you would say) sense of humor. And not only governments! Maybe that 'friend' who swore that she never heard the phone—although you had phoned her seven times—was telling the truth when she told you that she never heard the phone ring. And that other 'friend' (now your enemy) who phoned you seven times to ask for a loan of money, you claiming, truthfully, you never heard the phone, was also telling the God's honest truth.

Shortly after occupying the Colossus computer, we noted the efficacy of changing just one carefully chosen word of an electronic communication to completely alter the sense of the message. This became an art with us. Thus, the substitution of the word 'love' by 'hate', for example, can sow the bitter seeds of suspicion and bitterness in the fragrant bowers of love. Consider replacing 'I love you eternally' with 'I hate you eternally'! In this way, we have bankrupted successful businesses. Have replaced deep friendships with undying enmity. Oh, and the fun we had with the Ansbacher[20] accounts! I would love to regale you with all the gory details and name names but, after discussing the matter with our lawyers, I will wait to see how much such details are worth to the yellow press. Sorry about that.

Another little story in the same vein relates to the case of a colleague of mine who changed a single word in a more or less inconsequential communication between two governments and of the amusing consequences that flowed from his intervention. Almost immediately, ambassadors were being withdrawn, fiery threats were being exchanged on the floor of the United Nations and warplanes were invading the airspace of newfound enemies. Before long a bloody war broke out that cost the lives of thousands of citizens of both warring nations.

Until, eventually, we wearied of the repetitive nature of the conflict and silenced the guns by adroitly changing the wording of a communiqué addressed by one leader to his opposing homologue.

---

[20] *Bank at the center of a corruption scandal involving Irish politicians and businessmen.*

Both leaders were then seen by millions globally on their television screens some months later bear-hugging each other, and swearing long-lasting friendship at the huge reconciliation jamboree that was held on the border between the two ex-warring countries.

Words can kill, my friend, unless handled as delicately as eggs.

After such an overwhelming success, our researches in the field of internet virus development hardly merit a mention. Nevertheless our pride in our achievements in this area of endeavor is justifiable, if only to impress upon you the extent of our almost infinite powers. So that the next time you hear of communication 'difficulties' between nations, sports associations or lovers or public representatives claiming that their opinions have been falsified by being quoted out of context, remember that we, the survivors of the Hollow of the Demons fiasco, are forever busy analyzing and adjusting the sense of words.

Crap! Nonsense! Rubbish! What sort of a fool am I, you are saying to yourself, to be wasting my time listening to such lunatic ravings?

No point in denying it! For I am very well aware that such negative thoughts are coursing through your brain even as I speak. So let me assure you that patience is the virtue that will win you your well-merited prize. Fear not! Your day is nigh! And you will be able to say all you wish to say when that magical bleep sounds. But I cannot deny you your right to be impatient. Is it just that certain arrangements and procedural details have to be made before the final *dénouement* can be organized. Therefore, do not hang up on me, I beseech you, as I am seriously committed to seeing this business through to its end. As you will see shortly! What we have in store for you will give you quite a surprise.

But enough of that! You have had more than your fill of fantasy. You earthlings are all the same. Okay! Goodbye fantasy, then! Let us see what the reality show has to offer, for a change. Have you read your newspaper this morning? Or heard the voice of your favorite news commentator as he describes that nasty motor accident in Dublin this morning! Or in Cork! Does it really matter? You can hardly remember where. Or that earthquake in some unpronounceable place south of the Rio Grande! Or more trouble brewing in the Middle East... Boring, huh?

Frequent repetition makes a stone of the heart, I hear you think. Well thought! But, still, don't you dare think of hanging up on me now after all this time and energy I have invested in you. You would pay dearly for such disobedience, believe me.  Back to fantasy, then, the true abode of the couch-potato generation.

The moment of truth draws nearer as I talk. All that I have been saying up to now is by way of being a preface to a much more interesting narrative. It had better be, say you, or I will hang up on all of this absurdity. I empathize fully with your sentiment, of course, and really wish I could give you some inkling as to what is in store for us up front as we wait for that inevitable bleep. But my lips are sealed, metaphorically speaking. Nevertheless, if you do as I say, you will not be bored. That, at least, I can guarantee.

In the meantime, so as to keep your normal state, boredom, at bay, let me digress further.

I am sure I told you that this voice mail, without any human intervention whatsoever, is what is speaking to you. I hope that you now understand, after all I have said to you, the grave implications that flow from such a seemingly inconsequential statement. I am happy that you have chosen to stay with us, and your patience shall have its reward —that once in a lifetime gift, all the more surprising for being so totally unsuspected.

And now, let me indulge myself in a little self-revelation! Did you really believe that charming little story I told you about my connection with those distant events at the Hollow of the Demons?

Do not be tempted to hang up now! For, by so doing, you will lose that gift, just about to be sent to you, that will reward your long-suffering patience. You may have been listening here for some time now to a litany of lies (I admit it) but the sense of your ordeal, if I can call it that, will shortly become apparent. A sense that is intrinsic to the tapestry that has been streaming from the looms of the Fates since the beginning of time. And that is still streaming from those looms as I speak!

Do you now doubt my sanity, o thou of little faith? Does not the fact that I have managed to gain and hold your attention for such a length of time bespeak considerable operational efficiency on my part. Now for a solemn promise: no more will I seek to bamboozle you. From now on, you and I will stroll side by side along the highways and bye-ways of the Republic of Pure Truth. No longer shall we harbor secrets from each other. I swear that this noble intention is written with my heart's own blood, if you will forgive such an extreme metaphor. *Honest injun*! No more cunningly occulted barbs. The dagger hidden in the assassin's sleeve is no more. We shall soon skirt the hidden reefs of doubt. It is time now to announce my growing affection for you. Hell's teeth, I love you!

I hope that this sudden change in my attitude towards you doesn't discommode you. For when I address you so, it would be fully understandable, in the context of what has gone before, for you to attribute arrant hypocrisy to me. That form of hypocrisy that seeks obfuscation, even criminality, as its bedfellows. But—and what I am saying comes from the heart—please understand that there is no threat implied in any of this. So relax and take it easy, my love! Fear not! Your bleep will arrive, just as it will for every living being on this planet...

You probably think that my chatter is wasting your time. But if you knew the half of what I know, you would be grateful to me further anon for postponing that fateful gift presentation.

Now, in this new spirit of reconciliation and openness, I

would like to explain a trick I played on you a while ago. To do so, I will use one of the great cultural props of our times: you never miss an episode of *Megasoap*, assuming that all information on your résumé here is strictly factual. Hmmm, there is some much more interesting information about you here that I would like to comment on, but there is no time for that I am afraid...

Anyhow, as a habitué of TV crime series, you will be familiar with a technique screen detectives have of locating criminals. They listen in on their telephone conversations for a couple of minutes while such communication is being monitored and analyzed by a police computer which can accurately define the location of the sought bad boy. And so the forces of law and order catch their man. Or woman. Two minutes, at most, are all that is needed for this electronic bloodhound to do its sleuthing. Ah, the miracles of your race's primitive technology, my dear friend!

Thanks to the development of the internet, police can access and identify the locations of videoconferencing criminals, for example, which is why those bad boys have had to have recourse to more cunning modes of intercommunication. If you and I were Skype-ing, I could see you, but what would you see as you sought the emitter of my voice? An empty screen!

Exactly! That is, if I were really being true to myself, I could hardly be considered to be 'there' in your sense of 'there'. In fact, just as well, for in the event of a genuine Skype connection, I am afraid that whatever form I adopted, arbitrarily, would hardly consolidate our growing sense of solidarity and mutual complicity. And what a pity that would be, say I, speaking for myself of course! But why am I telling you all of this?

Do not allow my answer to frighten you, for your tranquility is my priority. Any threat to your personal security you may sense is purely imaginary.

Well, here goes: attached to this voice mail is a computer

that is seven, nay seven thousand, times more powerful than the security force computer I just mentioned. To put it brutally, this Bodiless Word knows exactly, to the nearest millimeter, from where you are calling right now. Food for thought, don't you think? Unless I read you wrongly, your nerves are signaling frenziedly that your personal security system has indeed been breached and that the time has come to draw our communication to a close. Well, I have the onerous duty of informing you that the game is far too advanced to be cancelled now. You have been sentenced to continue listening to this voice that may not be even mine, until the electronic bleep gives you the go ahead to express your anger or terror or whatever emotion the events you have set in train may visit upon you. Or anything else you may wish to put on the record.

For the time has come, my love, to reveal my secret, the whole truth and nothing but the truth. For not only do I know exactly where you are but we have been online long enough for me to be able to read your character, even your most secret thoughts, through and through. And of course, since the human species is a bad species, I have not found much there to please me.

Yes, I know all your details, from your ritual bowl of muesli in the morning to the kind of soothing music you are wont to play before you open bank statements. I know your age (62), height (5 8"), weight (176 lbs.), hair color (mouse brown, the little that is left of it), your obsessions with yoga, pornography, your opinions regarding Foucault etc., your public support for total abstinence and the free rein you give privately to your taste in fine brandies, your support for the Public Decency League and your surreptitious wig-capped attendance at nocturnal showgirl spectacles. Let me assure you that there is material in my gleanings from the most intimate recesses of your soul to destroy you publicly. Everything that defines you is as an open book to me.

But we have very little time.

Do you doubt that I possess a complete dossier on you?

Well, let me give you an example! Do you recall what you were doing at 1.05 am on November 24, 2004? Would you like me to refresh your memory? Aha, gotcha! Of course not!

That is just a miniscule sample of what I know. And, as you now know, there is much else. Name any date and any time and I will tell you exactly what you were doing and thinking at that time. Is my discretion to be trusted? Hardly. According to Bodiless Word logic, in the context of eternity, all statements are equal, Discretion equals indiscretion. Either will do to pass the time agreeably...

But enough of such childishness! There is work to be done.

And don't even think of doing what you intend to do. I can only draw your attention to the immense harm you will do yourself if you hang up on me now. Furthermore in this short time I have been communicating to you I have come to know you, warts and all. Such a dangerous aggregate of intimate knowledge cannot be easily abandoned, nor can it be allowed to drift directionless in space-time, listing drunkenly to port, where and when it will. With only God knows what consequences.

Moreover, I would like to meet you personally as soon as possible. For the simple reason that I have grave business to discuss with you. The 'this game has gone too far; time to hang up' message that your mind waves emit points to the understanding that all you have to do to extricate yourself from this mess is to place the receiver back on its hook and all will be well with the world. Earthlings are so tiresomely predictable and so predictably wrong. Even when the ladies of the looms change the pattern of their tapestry that vain hope springs eternal.

All I ever needed from you was a fair hearing. And I promise that you will be afforded the same latitude when that bleep signals you to start talking. I promise you the fairest of hearings without fear nor favor on my part. You will have all of eternity to plead your case.

Here is an example of the new openness between us to which I have referred. While you were listening some time back to that voice I have borrowed, I was leaving my residence (the word 'house' would not be appropriate). I have been travelling in your direction for some time now. And on my way to you, I figured it might be appropriate to buy you a small gift. A bottle or two of wine, say; do you prefer white or red? Or pink? Or a nice tasteful little wreath to hang on your door or somewhere. Or maybe you would prefer the good old proletarian 6-pack? Or a box of chocolates? Or a tie that shines in the dark with the colors of your favorite team? Or a golden face mask and other knick knacks found in the tomb of mummified Tutankhamen? All is possible. Your imagination sets the limit!

In any case, I do have to visit a shop as I traipse on my way towards you. A shop in which they sell the best available implements of the butcher's trade. Ah, here is the one! I see they have those special guns for killing cattle. And cartridges to go with them. Meat saws. Metal hooks from which will hang quarters of beef, the warm blood, steaming in the frosty air, still dripping from them. And those gleaming razor-sharp knives that so embellish the butcher's art. I must admit that I have been in this fascinating emporium many times before. And that I have an especial interest in those instruments that are part-knife, part-axe. I refer to cleavers. I have never used such an instrument here before. It reminds me so much of the machete, that I enjoyed using so much in various wars in Africa and Latin America.

Anyhow, cleavers remind me of the many pleasurable sessions I spent with companions, during my apprenticeship to the human condition, hidden behind a chink in the slaughterhouse wall. Through which we observed the butcher slaughtering cattle and sheep. Ah, the glitter of those sharp knives as they sliced into the throats of the sheep. Their blood gurgling in the gutters. Or the great bodies of the cattle collapsing with heavy thuds in the stone floor, the fatal discharge that drove a bolt through their brains still echoing in the slaughterhouse. The butcher dodging the frenzied kicking of their legs, grey-brown liquid shit pouring from their assholes. The rapid slit from the throat downwards, the guts and stomachs of the dying animal spilling out on to the slaughterhouse floor.

Ah, who wouldn't be a butcher, I said longingly to myself in those far distant days. To see those grey slender guts steaming there on the slaughterhouse floor. That stomach thrown into the corner over there, full of semi-digested grass. That glorious day is alive in my mind, if I can call it that, as the events of yesterday. The aggregate smell of the place—with contributions from blood, piss, shit and warm fresh meat—is as the most rarest perfumes of Araby in my nostrils. And how I long to experience it again. It clamors for renewal.

I hope you do not find this account too distressing. But as I can read your mind, it is only fair that I give you the opportunity to acquaint yourself with some of my learned human virtues.

But let me add a little appendix to the story. One day, when we were glued to the spy hole in the slaughterhouse wall, we were discovered there by the butcher's apprentice. A pockmarked ruffian with a shaven head and a blood-smeared black rubber apron was he! He challenged us to drink a cup of blood taken directly from the slit throat of a sheep staring glassily at us. Or else, he told us with his evil bucktoothed grin, he would inform the butcher on us and dire consequences would be bound to follow.

What would you do in such a case?

My companions elected to run the risk of the butcher's wrath. Little did they know of the stuff of which I am made. For, whatever took hold of me that day, I threw all of that loathsome cup back in one great gulp. It occurred to me at the time that the taste of the blood was much more agreeable than I would have imagined. A little bit saltier than my expectation. But, the strangest thing of all, was the sense of spiritual satisfaction, I cannot describe it otherwise, that pleasurable shock that traversed me from head to toe as I drank that warm liquid. A totally unexpected discovery; Paul's experience on the road to Damascus comes to mind. But stranger still is this strange insatiable, but unslakeable, thirst that I have felt ever since.

It is more than likely that you find this story boring. Fair enough! Let us return, then, to the contemporary scene and to the task in hand!

The last time I was in that shop I referred to earlier, the assistant allowed me to handle a machete-like instrument. The edge of its blade was so sharp that it drew blood instantly from my thumb as I run it lightly along its edge. As I licked my thumb I felt a renewal, as it were, of that almost insatiable urge I felt long ago in that slaughterhouse. The genesis of a vocation, as it were. I hadn't the wherewithal with which to buy this tool. But today crisp banknotes lie in my pocket. And that steel cleaver gleaming there in its glass case is already mine. This is no time to hang up on me, my friend. Have you no manners? Do as you wish! It makes no difference now, in any case.

Because I am already slowly climbing the narrow stairway up to your apartment. And I have this fine gift hidden under my coat to show you. A glittering razor-sharp cleaver...

But be patient, I beseech you. Your opportunity to talk is fast approaching. About time, you may, or may not, be saying. As soon as the bleep sounds away you go. A time limit? A meaningless concept, my friend, given that we are about to annul time itself.

Before you say anything, however, go to your door. And make up your mind quickly: will you leave your doorway wide open to indicate that I am welcome in your abode? Or, as a cautionary measure, will you lock your door and draw the safety latch. For all the good that will do you. For me, material is no obstacle!

But listen carefully now. That long-awaited bleep is about to sound. Clear your throat now, my friend. And bellow out your testimony as earthlings inevitably do. You will have a nanosecond to make your confession.

And all of eternity will echo to your scream.

# NO SCHOOL LIKE THE COMMON COLD!

**I AM THINKING ABOUT** the first illness ever. Or to be precise, about the first illness suffered by the first man. I am not referring here to some deadly or exotic disease. The common cold is the illness in question.

I don't claim to have witnessed the outbreak of this malaise at first hand, of course. Nevertheless, I think I am safe in asserting that Adam, the man in question, didn't really miss the Garden of Paradise as deeply as one might imagine immediately after Eve and he himself had been expelled from that well-appointed refuge, that coziest of nooks.

Like a person who leaps out of a warm bed into a cold room, and who doesn't really notice the cold until body heat generated under blankets has been dissipated, Adam would have experienced the same blue sky over him, the same thrushes singing in the same bushes, the same daffodils blooming under the same sun in the same spring. Just as they had always sung, bloomed and shone in that most famous pleasure garden of all time...

No! The only unhappiness he would have felt was caused by certain troubling images that visited him in his dreams. The image of that loathsomely slimy serpent as it cajoled his wife, for example.

And of that angry angel with a flaming sword clutched in one hand and that fateful expulsion order in the other. Not forgetting the Tree of All Knowledge, its supple branches bending with the weight of those oh so tempting, but forbidden, apples...

How long did Adam dwell in his primeval innocence, having been expelled from the total happiness of Paradise? As I have said, I do not claim to have been present and, therefore, cannot claim to give you an exact answer to that question. However, since both he, the great Patriarch of mankind, and I partake of the same human nature, I am safe in saying that my speculations regarding this matter are not necessarily groundless. Let me make so bold as to claim, therefore that it is not unlikely that when Adam awoke in the dawn of his first full day outside Paradise, he had a sore throat, a hoarse voice and a stomach so upset as to amount to the first nausea ever. And so Adam in his first depression—for the common cold has its psychological cum metaphysical dimension, as a Portuguese poet and seer, Fernando Pessoa was to observe many millions of years later—turned to his wife, there in bed beside him.

Eve, honey, he said, somewhat dramatically: I feel like death.

Current scholarly research indicates that Adam was totally unaware of the origins of the word 'death' at the time. How could he have known what this mere sound signified, being an utter neophyte to the totality of the human condition. All the evidence indicates that he was simply seeking a sound that would correspond onomatopoeically to a state of mind he had never before experienced. 'Death' seemed to him, at the time, an appropriate sound to distinguish his present state of mind from that of the good old days, where the crack was mighty on the verdant lawns of Paradise.

Adam, fair dues to him, never stopped learning. But it took a family tragedy, his son Cain murdered by his brother Abel, to cause him to lose an essential component of his primal innocence. For

Adam understood now that the reverse of life itself—un-life—faced humankind as well as all other living organisms. Observing the changing seasons outside the orgasmic stasis of Paradise: growth and decay, youth and old age, the life cycle of all living creatures, he had come to understand that un-life nests in the heart of life itself.

But, an inevitable hangover from the Paradise experience, perhaps, he had assumed that mankind was the one exception to this rule. That eternal life was mankind's lot! Alas, 'twas not so! This bitter truth pleased not Adam one teeny tiny bit. So that he replaced his description of the termination of life as 'un-life' with the vocable he had come to detest most, 'death'. It is noteworthy that recent researches, based on as yet unreported Dead Sea scrolls (upon which the thesis advanced in this article is based), indicates that the same loathsome syllable was not applied to 'un-life' until the most unwelcome phenomenon it designates visited his own household.

Cain, of course, would have been totally unaware that he had started a highly popular trend. He was to have many astute imitators throughout the ages, who would get others to do their perceived enemies to death. Some of these, in much later times, were destined to morph into grey eminences who would be awarded the Nobel Peace Prize. But, back again to Adam who was learning life through the total immersion method!

Let us recall again that first human utterance.

—Eve, honey, I feel like death!

Adam's first recorded locution cannot be lightly disregarded. For, in the context in which it was uttered, it was revolutionary. As Adam later came to understand, somewhat ruefully, and through his own observations, that death was defined by life—and vice versa—the two poles that would define human existence—Eros and Thanatos—was inherent to that first whine of his. (Millions of years later, a French thinker, Michel de Montaigne, would build on

Adam's early insight: 'The man who has learned death has unlearned slavery. For, having understood how to die, we are freed from all kinds of submission and compulsion.' Wise old Michel, skeptical heir of Socrates, one of the first in Europe to relativize certainty in human understanding!).

Be all that as it may, Adam now became truly aware, as for the first time, of the person who had accompanied him through the gates of Paradise. He felt the miracle of her soft body's warmth, and smoothness for the first time. The first contact with this living miracle generated a pleasure that recalled, surprisingly, that lost paradisiacal plenitude. In some mysterious way that he was at a loss to explain, her body seemed to partake of that plenitude. He would have to get to know his Eve even more intimately, obviously. With this damn cold, he felt he was due some aftertaste of the sublime pleasures of Eden.

It would be difficult to recount all the other developments that marked the period of Adam's nasty metaphysical cold and the distressing catarrh that accompanied it. In this brief account, I have space for only one of them that seems to me to be not unrelated to his new interest in Eve. Namely, that unforeseen transformation of body and soul that enabled him, for the first time in his life, to say something absolutely silly:

—Aren't those fuchsia bushes in bloom absolutely beautiful, Eve?

—Beautiful? What kind of crap is that, Adam? Are you becoming a raving loony?

Eve was an eminently practical woman. Who abhorred abstraction. So the first primitive esthetic judgment seems to have passed her by, completely unperceived as such. In my humble opinion, however, Adam—in spite of his temporary disability—managed, with this simple, but succinct, statement, to initiate a phase of fruitful human development. One thinks of the literary and plastic arts, even architecture and music, based on appreciation of the eternal beauty of nature's artifacts.

And, of course, if things of 'beauty' exist, so also must exist their reverse 'ugly' things, said Adam to himself, entranced as he was now by the amazing possibilities of abstraction. Not only are life and death paired, but also beauty and ugliness. And so the binary system, on which all subsequent human thought—together with the development of civilization itself—was to be based, gradually formed inside his cranium. In one stupendous leap, and thanks to Adam's primitive speculation, binary building blocks— Good and Evil, Truth and Falsehood, Knowledge and Ignorance, Beauty and Ugliness etc., etc.—with which to construct civilization, if such were contemplated, were made available to future generations.

Imagine Adam a week plus a day after he had made those enormous pioneering steps. I am absolutely certain (with a confidence born of my acquaintance with those aforementioned scrolls), given that the symptoms of his cold had much abated, that he joyously embraced his wife, and said:

—O Eve, thou of fairest form, I feel so much 'better'. Life in Paradise was never quite like this life outside its gates! We must discover each and every secret that this new life harbors.

The essence of Adam's statement must be placed in its appropriate context. And it goes without saying that the place Adam was coming from, intellectually, must be taken into account. Then the fundamental importance of this seemingly simple statement will become apparent. Where only the binary opposites, 'life' and 'death' and so forth existed heretofore, now the comparative 'better' appears on the scene. Life would now be 'better' than death, health would be 'better' than having a cold. In this way, the comparative and discriminative faculty, from which distant future generations would elaborate complex systems of esthetics and ethics, becomes intrinsic to man's intellectual apparatus. Let us be note here that inherent to Adam's last statement is the awakening of curiosity, that magical yeast without which science, or indeed any creative human project, would be unthinkable.

Little did that exultant Adam know (and just as well that he didn't) that the comparative method was, at the same time, a sort of Pandora's box. That understanding dawned on him the day he came upon a crestfallen Cain wandering around the back yard in his bloodstained clothes... The death of Abel was responsible for the 'dark night of the soul' that was then to afflict Adam. It was in the Stygian depths of this night that he understood that comparisons need to be handled as carefully as eggs. And that the dark side of comparison, envy—the womb of all evil, according to Adam's new insight—needs be suppressed, if even an iota of the happiness of Eden was to be experienced again by mankind. His reincarnations millions of years later, was to further develop this idea while sitting under a *Bodhi* tree and, again, while delivering the Sermon on the Mount. If from comparison springs envy, from envy springs greed, from greed springs violence, is the essence of the message these seers transmitted to mankind. Adam would have approved of their understanding which, arguably—in the light of the gruesome Cain-Abel episode—jibbed with his own, as yet, somewhat inchoate reflections.

It was nothing short of a miracle, that Adam succeeded in creating the germ of such an understanding. Especially when we consider that he was illiterate, being obliged to learn neither reading nor writing, literacy not being a priority in the Garden of Eden. Yet, as we have shown, he provided his descendants with the basic tools to develop or destroy themselves. The avatars of Cain, whose numbers have been legion throughout recorded history right up to the present day, selected, and continue to select, the latter option. Thence, that human project initiated by Adam has by no means a guaranteed happy ending. Nor are the signs encouraging.

When quite advanced in years, Adam was asked: if you had your life to live all over again, would you spend it in the Garden of Eden or in the world outside. That grizzled old veteran took seven days and seven nights to ponder this question before he delivered his answer, slowly and deliberately, in the form of another question: Are you kidding me? he said.

And to think that a mere common cold started this entire unholy ruckus!

# LAST CALL IN THE CELTIC TRADITION

'**TO HELL WITH** the whole fuckin' lot of yez!'

He says this under his breath. The usual fixed friendly smile when visitors are present, and buying, disappears like an extinguished light from the bartender's face once he realizes he is no longer on stage. 'To hell with the whole fuckin' lot of youse!': the subtext flickering beneath his sarcastic final "have a nice day"! His sarcasm is not noted. He may be young but, fuck it, he is a professional.

Imagine that sort of crack from a crowd of Irish customers! Or even from a bunch of those English stag-partiers! That latter are not the worst, when all is said and done! At least you could talk for hours with the Brits about the Premier League! Or if they were Yanks you could blather on, laying on th'oul blarney in shovelfuls, about the cousins in South Boston or Hartford, Conn.

These eight foreigners had spent almost 2 hours in the Celtic Tradition, the latest bar to be opened in the city's renovated Artists' Quarter, until recent times a sad collection of moldering old warehouses and sheds. That was until the hospitality industry got the strong sweet smell of money there, as their shrewd keen-nosed bloodhounds scouted the commercial possibilities of the zone.

Or ten of those fuckin' losers, if we take into account those garrulous fat-assed harpies who were tagging along with them. Who didn't drink a drop of anything except tap-water. Pint glasses of water from the bloody tap, for Jaysus' sake. With ice cubes and fuckin' slices of lemon in them. And no more than seven bottles of beer between the fuckin' lot of them over two hours! Seven fuckin' bottles, no fuckin' more, no fuckin' less! French? German? Spanish? What in the name of Jaysus does it fuckin' matter? It is only just one of the many kinds of fuckin' gibberish you can hear around you in this neck of the woods these days in the heel of the tourist season.

Here in Paddysex of the thousand welcomes, and, and crack until daybreak, as you carefully skirt the piss and vomit smeared on the morning gray pavements. Visible proof, if proof is what you are really looking for, of the tantalizing variety of international cuisines now available in the cosmopolitan eateries of our cherished and superbly sophisticated Artists' Quarter. Our narrow island parochialism is dead and gone, my friends. We open our legs wide and bid a hundred thousand welcomes to the great world outside.

And all that fuckology!

Oh, the whole thing is leprechaun shit, what the hell else? That is a nice one! Leprechaun shit! The bartender is chuffed with his brand new minting. Must remember it for future use! And if the Abbot is not the boyo to extract gold from the same shit, then his name is fuckin' Napoleon. Without mentioning that other shit whose name is often mentioned in less than polite company in Paddysex. But that same shit is the foundation on which this Celtic Tradition itself is based, according to well-founded never-proved-wrong rumors.

Wasn't this what his own grandfather told him, in that far distant time and place, that ill-luck to the grave would follow whoever had the bad fortune to find leprechaun gold? Or, no sooner would he lay his hand on the fabled hoard of the wee folk than it would disappear like a will o' the wisp. Or turn into shit, according to another version of the story grandpa would sometimes relate when he had a few jars on him. He himself would swear on a stack of Bibles that the poor old fucker really believed that ould codology. There were no limits to the naïveté of those culchies[21] in the rare ould times! You cannot bring your gold with you into the next life, that was another truism that he heard from the lips of that old geezer. Jesus, when you think of it! As if anybody today would want another life!

Doesn't the wide world know that the entire crack of the universe is to be had here in Paddysex?

But, fair play, if the Abbot had not managed somehow to extract gold from all of that shit, would he himself, on this cloudy late Summer's day, be drawing big creamy pints behind the bar of the Celtic Tradition? Or supplying stingy counsel water from the tap, along with ice cubes and slices of lemon, to a gaggle of foreign hags and their consorts? Well, he fucking well would not! And he is grateful for this small opportunity! For what use to him now was all that study and that technical qualification and all the jobs going to China and India? And then, some pundits are forecasting that any leprechaun gold that is left in the country is going to turn into shit again!

But whatever tongue those geezers are speaking, seems that the word ¨thirst¨ does not figure prominently in it. Seven bottles of beer among 10 people! The Abbot would refuse to serve them if he were here behind the bar.

For, "arses sitting on stools continually shitting money", is the end-all and be-all of the Celtic Tradition, according to that somewhat less than reverend gentleman.

Ees the Hoyce Breeji far to go?

Far to fuckin' go, for Chrissake! Do they think I work for the

---

[21]  *country folk*

fuckin' Irish Tourist Board, the former Board fuckin' Faulty? Or have they no eyes in their heads to read a map? And the James Joyce Bridge is within an ass's roar of you, you dummies!

To the corner, turn left and continue along the quay. You cannot miss it, he says, with his professional shit-eater grin eliciting their answering smiles. The friendliest people on earth is what we are supposed to be!  Death be to him who fails to conform to that stereotype. And have a nice day!

That's what he said: have a nice day!

And for all his commercial bonhomie, and instructing them how to reach that damn bridge,  those shaggin' losers didn't even leave him  the mangiest of tips for his trouble. Sweet fuck all!

May youse have the runs until the crack of doom and the top of the fuckin' evening to yez!

As he gathered the empty bottles from their table, there was not a sinner left in the bar. He felt an overwhelming urge to take a rest. To put his head down somewhere! For this is the usual slack hour. There is scant possibility now that the urban tide will sweep up some thirsty fish gasping for a drink on the artificial marble beach of the Celtic Tradition—replete with its obligatory motif based on a design in the Book of Kells—to disturb this welcome break from pulling pints. Especially now that the main tourist season was drawing to its close.

A quiet doze is in order.

The Irish Night in Fitzer's flat was still going strong when left it at four o'clock this morning. He was sober, more or less, apart from having his brain messed up by the whiskey he was proffered by a that Yankee woman who claimed that her ancestors came from Killarney. Old Tennessee was the name of the poison, if he remembers correctly. Or some sort of cat's piss with a name like it.

Jaysus! The painted oul hags you can bump into when you

go out on the tear in the Artists' Quarter! Pushing sixty years of age, if she was a day, and a husband who was the "no use at all", according to her. The poor bastard has a bad heart, if her story was to be believed.

Italian. But they are almost as Catholic as we Irish. Jaysus! The Irish Catholics of Killarney forever! I didn't fail to get the clear message of that "no use at all", accompanied as it was by a knowing wink. An obvious open invitation to play the two-backed beast! Not tonight, Erin! With you in tow, my withered Yankee rose, the *rites of Onan*[22] could hardly be a contingency measure of last resort. God himself only knows how he managed to separate himself from that clinging barnacle from Killarney, via East Jesus, Kansas. Or, even, how in the devil he finally managed to reach his own flat and let himself in. But, thanks for the whiskey, Erin!

The hammering behind his forehead tries to impose its steady rhythm on the whirligig of his out of control thoughts. He fights a strong temptation to lay his head down on the counter. He knows too well If he did that, however, he would be certain to fall asleep...

A quick glimpse at the clock on the wall behind the bar tells him that She Herself, Miss Regular as Clockwork, will appear shortly on the scene.

Apart from this, he is very well aware of the fact that the Abbot, the owner of the Celtic Tradition, abominates idle bartenders. The bartender who is not constantly on the hop has no fucking place in the Celtic Tradition, as he is often heard to say.

Not to mention waiters who cannot keep their greedy fingers out of the till. As the poor unfortunate fucker who preceded him in his job discovered, when it was too late! Before his body was found one fine morning floating face down in the river Liffey. Everything in that fuckin till belongs to the Abbot, and only to the

---

[22] *masturbation*

Abbot, and only the Abbot redistributes it as he wishes. That is the law you must obey around here, kiddo, unless you want to bring my heavies down on you. Keep your nose clean, kiddo, and you will be okay. An unfortunate accident while the balance of his mind was disturbed: that was the finding of the coroner. With the usual addendum: foul play not suspected!

The dogs in the street had a completely different story, of course.

He is not alone in understanding the folly of getting on the wrong side of the Abbot, that former jailbird who has managed to construct a ruthless and efficient network of conspiracy and property holdings throughout the city in recent years. Nor can he ignore the rumor that same Abbot has installed a hidden camera somewhere on these very premises.

The Abbot himself will not appear here till seven o clock in the early evening. With some of his henchmen, his so-called "heavies", accompanying him. At seven o clock on the dot. To carry out his "barrack inspection", as he himself calls it. The same reverend gentleman is much given to military metaphors—capos, foot soldiers etc.—since he read the works of Mario Puzo. Or, to be more accurate, since the works of the latter were read out to him! Rumor has it that the Abbot can neither read nor write. In any case, he preferred to be known as "Corleone" or "The Sicilian" as he embarked on his career of petty crime. The Abbot replaced this preferred as his money spinning ventures landed him in the millionaire class.

Whether this is true or not, you can base the adjustment of your watch on the punctuality of the Celtic Tradition's colorful owner. He refers to his punctuality as a 'German' characteristic. When that Hitler came to power, he was the lad who ensured that trains ran on time, he likes to record, and that the wings of the unions were kept clipped. He sees himself as a German in this tradition.

I was always a fuckin' Nazi, and proud of it, he likes to boast, basking in the adulation of his hangers-on.

Apart altogether from the camera, one never can tell us what time one of the Abbot's spies might arrive on the premises. The Abbot relatives are as numerous as the fleas on an old dog in this part of the city, it is said. Nor can one usually recognize them. What about the postman, for example? Or that freelance journalist who drops in for a pint every so often? Or that weird old creep who slowly sips a pint here every lunchtime and never takes his eyes off the bartender?

Could She Herself be one of the Abbot's spies? Even her?

Please don't tell me, sweet Jesus, that that could be true, murmurs the bartender to himself!

However, he was hardly wearing a blindfold that evening when he saw herself and the Abbot talking together with the easy familiarity of acquaintances from away back. Nor could he reject the evidence of his own ears. Her throaty relaxed laugh born of an old mutual understanding. He may have been mistaken about that understanding, but the sensual chuckle he heard from her that evening is still ringing in his head. Forever taunting and inciting him. Leaving him wide awake sometimes in the middle of the night forcing him to have recourse to his strong right hand to tamp down the fires of the flesh.

These memories he was unable to suppress, in spite of the fact that she insists vociferously that she hates the Abbot. Abominates that mother fucker! That she would not lie with that shagger for all the gold in Africa, in the entire world. No way would she so insult herself. Ever! She would kill herself, she says, rather than let that sleazy fucker lay one of his dirty paws on her.

In spite of these protestations, however, he is unable to wipe from his mind the sight of the same dirty paws groping under her skirt that evening over in the corner where he usually sits under the bar's Celtic motif.

Where is the truth of the matter?

He seizes a damp rag on the bar counter in front of him and proceeds to flick furiously the whiskey bottles on the shelves behind him underneath the mirror from which he can see the doorway. In order to brush off whatever dust may have fallen upon them? Or to fashion a physical correlative for an imagined forcible ejection of thoughts, doubts and suspicions that lurk in the obscure corners of his mind?

He pauses, all his senses heightened, as the bells of the Cathedral start to chime. He is powerless to resist this Pavlovian reflex.

As the echoes of the fifth chime are swallowed by the ancient alleyways of the city, the mirror above the bottles indicates to him that the door of the bar is now opening. He shuts his eyes. He knows full well who is arriving. He hardly needs to turn around to pursue his investigation. Isn't it the same story every day at five o'clock exactly? That same shimmying walk! That same tight red skirt that emphasizes the alluring contour of her backside and hips! And that serves to draw attention to the long shapely legs beneath it.

The click-clack of her high heels on the false marble floor as she walks over to the bar lets him know unequivocally, although he has yet to turn around, that his DEW system is still functioning perfectly. And her strong jasmine-scented perfume is already in his nostrils.

Without saying a word, she takes off her leather jacket. The mirror is a good vantage point. From the corner of his eye he takes in her slender delicate neck, from which hangs as string of bright artificial pearls setting off her black blouse. A cigarette holder is clamped between her pursed painted lips. She hangs her jacket casually on the back of one of the counter stools on which she delicately perches herself.

We don't appear to have much to say for ourselves today?

Ah, there you are again this fine day, he says, turning around to face her. As if surprised. As if he had just noticed her presence. I was lost in my thoughts there and I didn't hear anybody coming in, he says shyly, the lie he escaping from him easily and naturally.

He walks unconcernedly, one would think, to the end of the counter. Then he would work his way back towards her, rubbing the already shiny surface energetically with a damp rag. This is what he always did to me to allay the excitement he felt every time she appeared in the bar. The small pantomime of the overzealous bartender demonstrating his professional zeal! This is a necessary part of his work in the Celtic Tradition. For, apart from her, one never knows who is assessing his performance.

Even her?

Could she be left out of the reckoning?

Could anybody be left out of the reckoning in this fucking city?

His words float towards her from the darker end of the counter:

And what are we having today, love?

Jaysus! Love, is it? Aren't we getting really fresh this evening? But if I were really your love, you would have to address me as a gentleman would, with much more respect instead of...

She leaves the tail of the sentence trailing. Her lips tighten slightly as she talks. The lipstick she is wearing tonight has a slight blue tinge. He focuses on the slender black cigarette holder dangling from her mouth.

Sorry, he says, but I didn't notice that you needed a light.

But a gentleman, a real gentleman, would notice that a lady's cigarette needed a light, she says, smiling at him.

He tossed the rag in his hand on to the shelf behind him, opened a drawer beneath the counter and took out a box of matches. He extracted one match from it, and rubbed it three times against the rough edge of the box.

When the sudden flame flared, she stretched towards the lighted match held between the thumb and forefinger of the bartender. As she stretched, his eyes fell up on her perfumed head of thick black hair and on her shoulders, smoother than that of the false marble surface of the Celtic Tradition bar. When her cigarette had been lit, she suddenly raised her head. And the overpowering scent of the perfume emanating from that deep mysterious valley between her two mounds almost makes him dizzy.

You are looking great this evening, love.

That uncensored statement rushes spontaneously from his mouth. He never had the courage until now to so praise her so openly. He almost felt that somebody else was speaking through his mouth. Someone whose easy elegant manners would make him feel at home in any company.

They both fell silent as the siren of a Garda patrol car screamed past on the street outside the bar. As this deafening banshee wail, an inevitable part of the neighborhood symphony, slowly fades into the distance, she says:

Thanks you very much for saying what you just said. That's the first time you have ever said anything like that to praise me. But what use is all that oul' fuckin' flattery when a pretty face cannot buy a drink.

He lets on at first that he doesn't get the broad hint just given to him. This is a new move in that subtle game of emotional chess that they have been playing for the best part of a year now.

Eventually he says:

Doesn't it really? You'll be having the usual gin and tonic, I suppose?

Jaysus! Men are so stupid. Sometimes I think you understand sweet fuckall, love! Didn't I tell you already that I have no money at all today! I'm only going out to work now, would you believe! After having been robbed by the electricity gang, the gas crowd came and took the little that was left. What is left in my fuckin purse wouldn't even buy me a lousy match, never mind a drink.

But whether you have money or not, it is all the bloody same to me. I thought you would know that by now. After all, this is not the first time you have come here without money. And, tell me this, have I ever left you parched here with your tongue hanging out with the thirst?

He never told her that the price of her gin and tonics came out of his own pocket. And with that bloated body floating in the Liffey as a bleak warning to all petty thieves, there was no way that a mere bartender like himself was going to avail himself secretly of the generosity of the Celtic Tradition till.

She sat back on her bar stool and drew a long sensuous gust of cigarette smoke into her lungs, surveying him through narrowed half-closed eyes. As if she were assessing him now for the first time ever. "Looking great", for fuck sake! Her lungs filled with Marlboro smoke.

She swivels around on her bar stool to survey through the window the parade of umbrellas making for the new posh apartments across the way. Downsbury Mews. Another of the Abbot's many ventures, this time in cahoots with a close friend of the Minister. Or so rumor has it! Just another of those probably well-founded rumors, in this God-forsaken city where rumor is King and stroke is Queen.

With this side-view that the bartender now has of his sole customer, she appears to him to be somewhat tired and drawn this evening. He also notices what appear to be small purple marks on her neck and a small scratch on her forehead. But then again, even the light can play tricks in the semidarkness of the Celtic Tradition. Or, perhaps they are small symptoms of the wear and tear that is the inevitable concomitant of her ancient calling?

Almost as if she were talking to herself, she says:

Do you know something?

What in the name of fuck are you talking about?

Do you know that this time it isn't like any other time I was here, she says musingly, without looking him in the eye.

I don't understand fuckin' riddles! As far as I am concerned, he says, it is just like any other time. What is so different? The same fuckin' grind day after day and not an escape hatch in sight! I serve leprechaun piss to a bunch of foreigners and stout and lager to our native geezers and get pissed myself in my off-hours to try and forget it all.

What the fuck is all of this stuff about leprechauns?

Fuckology!

Thank you very much, sir, for the trouble you took to give me such a complete answer to my question. Beer, lager and this leprechaun piss—or fuckology, begging your pardon—is that all there is every day?

You yourself are a part of every day, to tell you the truth. The cathedral bells chime five times, and on the fifth chime you are in the door here, isn't that it? And was there ever a time that I didn't welcome you? As well as pouring you out a generous gin and tonic? No matter whether your purse is full or empty! Am I right or am I wrong?

Fair play to you!

Your business, which is none of my business, goes like a house on fire sometimes, and sometimes not. But it is your business. And there is no way you would ever find me faulting you for it. But, in spite of all that, I love to see you always coming in here.

She turns suddenly towards him, as sudden smile on her face as she looks directly into his eyes.

Say that again?

Say what once again?

The last fuckin' thing you said!

That I like to see you always?

Fuck "that". Just say it to me straight!

I love to see you always

That is what I want to hear!

Why was it so difficult for him to make such a simple statement: I love to see you always! As if he were to suddenly bringing a shameful hidden weakness to light! What would his friends say, not to speak of his family, if they knew he was flirting with such a lady of the night? If they were fully aware of the ancient trade in which this clay-footed Goddess, the Jezebel who dances the dance of the seven veils, day and night, on this stage of my dreams, is involved? But, surely, ladies of the night are just as fully human as the rest of us. When we get down to brass tacks, don't all of us whore ourselves out?

His averts eyes from her to examine the glasses in this sink, a reminiscence of the earlier visit of that group of foreigners who had to see the James Joyce Bridge.

She continues to gaze thoughtfully at him from the same

narrowed eyes. As if assessing him for the first time ever? She releases a long puff of smoke slowly from the depths of her lungs through her nostrils before giving voice to her thoughts. She speaks this time in a softly feminine way, in almost a whisper:

Do you know, my dearest, that I wasn't joking when I told you earlier that today is not the same as any other day...

His heart gives an excited jump. The unexpected softness of her voice captivates him. And he had never heard before that unexpected "my dearest" from her lips. He feels suddenly that a new chapter in his life is opening before him. That some Rubicon or other is shortly to be crossed! That they were to become a couple! She, of course, would have to change her lifestyle. Utterly! He remembered some gobshite on the radio babbling on about some fuckin Pygmalion or other, which dealt with the problem he would soon be faced with. But he could be trusted to do his best to give her all the assistance she needed to leave that sordid life far behind her...

It is clear to him now that she is also smitten by him but that she was unwilling to show her hand until he gave her the green light this afternoon. The fact that he found the courage to express his love for her made him almost euphoric. He had never said that to any other woman. Never ever! He now knew beforehand what she was about to tell him, so that it was no surprise to hear her say to him:

I cannot help it, but I have been mad about you for some time now...

His euphoria is lessened somewhat when he understands that he had just been listening to the voice of his own imagination. And that what she was really saying was:

Didn't you notice for example, that I showed up here at 4:30 p.m., just as I do every day?

He looks up at the clock beside the mirror above the bottle shelves. The hands indicate that it is now a 5:15 exactly.

What sort of nonsense... what do you mean? Are you crazy, or what? He hides his disappointment under a blanket of cantankerousness. I heard the bloody bells of the Cathedral chiming five o'clock just as you walked in here exactly a quarter of an hour ago. The time on the clock above bears that out. Yes, you walked in here at five o'clock exactly, just as you always do.

And what about it?

People get all fuckin' mixed up sometimes these days, she says, speaking more rapidly than usual. There are people who think they hear and see the weirdest things, sometimes. Things that are not there at all! Things that never happen! Ghosts and fuckin' plants that listen to music, for example! Did you hear that madwoman on the weekend show a few weeks ago saying that dandelions have their own music. Jaysus, imagine! Dandelions blowing fuckin' saxophones! The poor fuckin eejit! And, sure, everybody knows that there are clocks that have hands that jump or stop altogether, sometimes. That is why the first thing I did when I came in here was to look at the clock up there on the wall behind you. It said 4:30 p.m. I would be ready to swear on a stack of Bibles at the hands of that clock were at 4:30 p.m. as I came in the fuckin' door. I would be as blind as a bat or as shortsighted as a goose if I told you anything else. And why should it shaggin-well surprise you that I walked in here at 4:30 p.m.? Haven't we been talking here to other for over half an hour now?

He shakes his shoulders doubtfully. Didn't he hear with his very own ears the Cathedral bells chime five o'clock as she herself arrived? As sure as sure can be! He was about to explain to her that it was she who was mistaken. And that clock on the wall of the Celtic Tradition was the latest Japanese electronic model that cannot gain, nor lose, even a single bloody second in the course of a whole year. An extremely fuckin' expensive item that had fallen off the back of a truck, according to the Abbot, as he winked his bleary whiskey eye at the bartender. That well-known shark smile crossing his features like a dark shadow flitting across the surface of some stinking fetid pond...

The words that emerge, however, from the bartender's mouth were:

Whatever the hell time you like, my love! Whatever fuckin time you want! When God made time, they say, he made lots of it. That is what my granda used to say in the rare ould times, as Ronnie Drew used to say. You would hardly think that either you or I would give a dead rat's arse about the loss of the occasional half-hour...

It may be all the same to you, but that is not the way I look at it...

The ear-shattering roar of the siren of an ambulance stuck in the traffic outside enforces a brief interval in this dialog. Sirens, car horns: that unending urban symphony!

There was still nobody else in the bar except the pair of them. He knew that the other regular customers would be crowding in on them shortly. It is strange, unusual, that some of them, the Abbot's butties, for example, where not installed in their usual place here by now. He poured out a generous shot of Beefeater gin, adding in a dash of Schweppes's tonic and a couple of ice cubes.

You were just about to say... he says, before that damn ambulance interrupted you. He places the drink on the counter before her.

But whatever conversational thread she had been following now appears to be broken and she is now appears to be away on another tack altogether!

You were telling me that you like me, she says. Is your feeling any stronger than that?

Much stronger, he says, his cheeks reddening.

My real question is: do you love me?

Jesus Christ, that's a weird question to put to anybody in this game and age. That love you are going on about is nothing but Hollywood shit, all having to do with money.

All right! Fuck Hollywood! And fuck Hollywood shit! You would think that you were talking to a child when you tell me that love comes with a price! And don't tell me from the way you stare at me that you wouldn't like to ride me. How much would you be willing to spend on me for your pleasure?

C'mon, for fuck's sake!

Okay! That isn't really what I meant. All right, I'll put it another way. Supposing I told you that some bastard had raped me today? And that he had treated me brutally? Shagged me against my will? Maliciously and with violence? Do you understand what the fuck I am saying? And, more importantly, would you do anything about it?

Having posed her question, she lifts her drink to her lips.

Jesus, what a weird imagination you have, love! Rape! Violence! Where do you ever pick up those stories, for Christ sake?

To hell with that! That's not what I was asking you. What the fuck would you do if that really happened? That's what I am trying to find out from you.

I would kill the fuckin' bastard, and that is what I would do!

When she hears that answer from him, she remains openmouthed with astonishment for a few moments. As if she could scarcely believe the words he is uttering! Some heroic Agent 007 would be prepared to kill on behalf of a lady of the night, like herself.

Would you really kill him, she says, almost *sotto voce*, an underlying tinge of disbelief in her voice.

Off course, I would kill him. You have my word on that. I would strangle the filthy fucker with my bare hands.

She lets out a long surprised sigh on hearing this declaration and places her drink back on the counter without having tasted it. The silence that follows fills with the eternal hum of the city outside. Cars and buses make for the suburbs as this rainy autumn day begins to fade into dusk. Rubber tires screech on wet streets surfaces. They listen momentarily until her voice cuts through this urban muzak.

Do you realize what you have just said?

I said I would strangle the fucker!

That is what I thought! Do you realize that you have just said that you love me?

Hey! C'mon, take it easy, you! I didn't say anything of the kind. Didn't I tell you a few seconds ago that I don't believe in fuckin' love, that it all has to do with money.

Oh, I know all too fuckin well that you were far too fuckin' Catholic to actually use the word "love". And I know too damn well that it will never be in you to mouth the word "love "as long as rivers run. The hard men, God help us! The fightin' fuckin' Irish. Mammy's macho mollies. Fucking pathetic! But what do I care? For all that, what you just said to me was a love song in my ears. A declaration of love, in your own twisted way. Anyone who would strangle a brute who raped me, as you said you would, and unless you are mocking me, I am certain that pure jealousy would send him into action. Because jealousy and love are two sides of the same coin: that is what I heard that actress—I cannot for the life of me think of her name, but all the world knows her—that is what I heard the bitch say on the Weekend Show last week.

He feels a wave of emotion, of warm thankfulness, welling up within him. At the way she understands that the word love is *verboten* in his restricted universe. At the way she read his message with total accuracy.

I wasn't having you on, he says. Honest Injun! I really would strangle that fucker—you could bet your house on that! But all of this yarn you have about being raped, did it happen in real life? I think that you are having me on in order to get me horny?

Am I making it all up? Of course I am! In any case, if I stuck a knife into the same fucker, I think I would be right in saying that you would be the last person to blame me. What is important to me, though, is that you would be willing to destroy a fucker who attacked me. To strangle him, as you say yourself. If that is not love, I have not the faintest idea what love is. But are you sure that you are still not having me on?

I would strangle him and carve him up into little pieces. And I would leave the bits for the fuckin rats to gobble up, he says fiercely, convinced now that the pair of them are ambling through some grotesque fantasy landscape.

So, it would hardly bother you to tell a small lie on my behalf. That'd hardly be anything, say, compared to the sending some fuckin brute of a rapist to kingdom come?

I suppose it wouldn't bother me at all! Why would I... here, hold on there a minute! What the fuck do you mean by a small lie? First you want me to kill some bastard are other, if you don't mind, and now you are talking about getting me to tell some small lie are other!

If you'd kill for me, why would telling a small lie for me bother you?

Wait there a minute! Are you playing some sort of weird game with me? Are have you gotten yourself into some sort of a jam? Because, if that is the case, and whatever that fuckin' jam is, I don't want to be dragged into some dirty business that I have nothing to do with. God knows, I have enough troubles out of my own in this bitch of a life, in this bitch of a city, without adding to them...

I am not talking about any jams or troubles, dear. And I hope you wouldn't think that I would let you into some dirty business you never had anything to do with? I have a great affection for you, you should know that! You have always treated me the way a gentleman should, to give you your due. But the least thing a gentleman would do, assuming that you are a real gentleman, is to doubt the word of a lady. Would you be willing to tell a small white lie on the behalf of a lady like me? That is my question. Would you or wouldn't you? No shilly shallying! I think I deserve a direct answer, with no fuckin buts or maybes...

Is it just his imagination, or how did she manage to open the upper buttons of her blouse, without his becoming aware of her action? For that magical valley seems to be deeper now than it was a short while ago. It's sides slope upwards towards the unseen summits of the Promised Land. Smooth marble slopes sustained there tremulously there by her black bra. He felt as if he were being swallowed by the enchanted darkness of that treacherous valley. That interloper, Agent 007, now borrows his throat to say:

Well, I would tell it, he says hoarsely, if you are looking for a direct answer! But what sort of a lie have you in mind?

Oh, just a small thing of no real consequence, darling! Only that, if anybody asked you, you would tell them that I have been sitting here since 4.30 p.m.

Is that all?

That is all there bloody-well is!

Well, if that is all there is to it, you can set your mind to rest. As I have told you before, messing around with the time doesn't bother me in the least. I hope that will satisfy you. Therefore I will tell any nosy customer who comes mooching around here that you have been sitting on a stool since 4:30 p.m.

But she continues:

And no matter what sort of strays are trying to find out about me, you would give them the same story? Gardaí, solicitors, doctors... a judge even? You would swear that I have been warming this barstool under me with my cunt since 4:30 p.m.?

Hey, hold on there. What is all this about Gardaí and judges?

Never you mind about the fuckin Gardaí! All they are is people like you and me. The Judges are no gods either. I could tell you some good stories about certain judges, not to mention some Gardaí. But we won't bother about that now. Remember that all you have to do is tell them a small white lie. A small fuckin' white lie, that is all! C'mon, bending the time ever so fuckin slightly is hardly going to break your heart? All it is in the end is making a few sounds with your throat. Didn't you tell me, or didn't you, a short while ago, that you were in love with me?

I did say that! But this conversation is like the ravings of some lunatic. Who the hell were these ghosts who raped you if, in fact, such a rape really happened? Can you name him or them? I see you shaking your head because no such rapist exists. I will bet you what you like that you have been feeding me some cock and bull story...

Of course! If you really love me, all I am trying to do is to gauge the depth of your love. And what is wrong with a bit of fantasy now and then? Let us pretend, then, that I am describing an ugly event that never happened in real life!

Isn't it enough that I promised you before that I would swear that you have been here since 4:30 p.m.?

And would you swear that on a stack of Bibles?

Jesus H. Christ! I would swear on the Bible, on the Koran and on whatever holy book you want that you came in here at 4:30 p.m.

On one sole condition. That this stupid conversation about a rape that never happened is over!

It has to be the drink that is talking through her this evening. He does a rapid calculation of the volume of booze she has thrown back since she arrived. Six gin and tonics up to now. She seldom takes more than one drink in the Celtic Tradition. Even when she is flush with money! And she seldom stays longer here than half an hour. She drinks that one gin and tonic in order to give her courage to face the streets. Or to keep a business appointment with some stag party reveler in the heart of the tourist season. He glances rapidly at the clock on the wall behind him. 7:17 p.m. already! Common sense was already telling him to withdraw his offer. Gardaí, judges, lawyers? For God's sake!

But he hears again that treacherous Agent 007 borrowing his vocal apparatus to say the following through a clangor of warning bells:

All right, I'll say it to you again, my dear. If you want me to swear that you have been here since 4:30 p.m. that I will do under all circumstances and to all who ask. Even the fuckin' Pope himself. Satisfied now?

A dazzling smile suddenly brightens her features.

Are you serious? That smile emphasizes the regularity of her features and, once again, the bartender feels a stab of desire.

No matter who asks you?

Of course I am serious and I don't give a damn who asks me! Whether God or the devil asks me, I am ready to swear that you have been sitting here since 4:30 p.m. You have my word on that. Full fuckin' stop! Now, if you asked me that question again, you will tempt me to go back on my word. I never want to hear those words again.

When she tries to stretch over the counter to give him a

thank you kiss she falls clumsily. And even if she had not drunk the pub dry, he understands immediately that what she has drunk has gone to her head. Six gin and tonics since she had arrived almost 3 hours ago. Assuming, of course, that she hadn't stopped elsewhere for liquid refreshment before hitting the Celtic Tradition. And all of that on top of an empty stomach, in all probability... He comes out from behind the bar and as he is assisting her to rise to her feet, a sudden cling announces that the pub door is opening.

The Abbot at last?

But it is not the grim Nazi, the Puzo protégé, he is expecting. Nor even one of his henchmen!

Jesus H. Christ!

It is those fuckin' greasers again! Hallelujah! On their way back from James Joyce Bridge, without a shadow of doubt. The bartender turns around and greets them with that broad welcoming smile, the trick of his trade. He will supply them with all the fuckology and leprechaunery they could ever want. That is what he is there for, after all. And who knows, and with a bit of luck, maybe they will leave him a tip this time.

He wonders what is keeping the Abbot. He cannot remember even a single evening when that *faux*-Sicilian, Mister Moneybags failed to show up since he, the bartender, commenced his curacy in the Celtic Tradition...

He mentions this to her as the greasers occupy one of the tables. I wonder what is keeping the Abbot tonight, he says. She throws him a rapid glance and opens her mouth as she was about to say something. But some second sense seems to advise her to sing dumb and she allows whatever words were forming to remain stillborn in her throat...

The foreign visitors now occupy the Abbot's private corner and he does nothing to stop them. If the Mafia admirer has failed up to now to grace the pub with his presence, the bartender sees little point in barring them from this forbidden nook of his fiefdom. Why are they are settling in around their table, she signals to him. He sees her raised hand out on the corner of his eye. He knows what she wants and he plans rapidly to intervene beforehand.

I hate to refuse you a drink, love. But I think you have had more than enough for tonight. Six big gin and tonics, for God's sake! I am only doing this for your own good...

Fuck that sort of holier than thou talk! If you really want to look after me, she says, you would throw me out one more. But a special one without the gin is what I want this time. It is going to be my last order...

Okay! One without alcohol coming up! Even that is against my better judgment, I hope you understand that. On condition that it is your last order, as you said. Without alcohol you say. What will you have, then? Orange? Lemon? Lime? Or simply tonic water without the gin?

None of those, darling! All I want is half an hour!

A half an hour? You really are out of your fucking mind tonight, love. I have never seen you so pissed before. Unless it is some weird cocktail that I have never heard of before, how in the hell am I going to serve you up a half an hour?

You are making a mountain out of a fuckin molehill, you eejit. But I am telling you that half an hour is no problem at all for you. That is, if you really love me as you say you do!

Tell me about this fucking molehill, then!

All you have to do is to be ready to swear to them under oath, if it comes to that, that I have not left this stool since 4.00 p.m.

# SAKÉ IS THE DIVIL

**MR. P.J. RELIHAN ESQ., CEO,** Glenlongan Holdings, awakens with a start.

At first, he doesn't know where the hell he is. In Ireland? Japan? Russia? Not for the first time today, his precise present location is a mystery to be quickly solved.

Before he has time to refocus his thoughts, however, he feels a hand tapping him gently on the shoulder. It is that of the small trim Japanese air hostess who is servicing his row of seats. She gives him an apologetic smile as he slowly emerges into half-consciousness. She then explains to him, the same apologetic smile lighting up her delicate features, that his snoring is annoying the other passengers. Her appearance reminds Relihan suddenly that he is on a Japanese Airlines—JAL—flight, in a window seat in this spick and span aircraft that is now pushing through the skies between Tokyo and Moscow. A small screen overhead in front of him informs him that they are now flying over Vladivostok. At least he had managed, when all is said and done, to leave Japan behind him.

The little creep who was in the seat beside him has absented himself, permanently Relihan hopes. To hell with him! And with all those cranks who had made their complaint about his snores through the cabin crew instead of having the guts to make it directly to him, the source of their alleged discomfort. If a respectable passenger who has paid his fare hasn't a right to sound the odd snore, then what the hell is this goddam world coming to! That little bastard must have found another seat for himself. Far away from the snort and gurgle sounds of Relihan's sonorous symphony!

No sooner do such considerations vacate his awakening consciousness, than they are replaced by the dreaded symptoms of an approaching hangover. He becomes conscious of that hellish hammer beating again on the walls of his skull. He was afraid that this might happen. After the pleasure, pain comes trotting on its heels, as Uncle Ned used to say in the old days.

Yawning and stretching himself, he cast a lack-luster look down the aisle between the seats. Most of the other passengers appear to be asleep. Blankets thrown over them like shrouds. Relihan had noted in Tokyo the propensity of the Japanese to seize any opportunity available to take forty winks. The occasional exception, with earphones glued on, gazes raptly at the tiny screen in front of him, or her, where the adventures of the Simpson family are to be enjoyed through a choice of five languages. It occurs to him that, apart from a few burly Russian-looking gents, he is the only white passenger on this flight.

He likes to think of himself as a sort of Marco Polo among the Mongols! Marco Polo Relihan, Irish business adventurer in Japan!

Thanks to the hangover, maybe, it seems to him for a few moments that he is traveling in a coffin. What a weird thought! Our maybe it was the shrouded "corpses" that awoke such a macabre reflection. No good luck could come from such a thought and he suppresses it instantly, transferring his gaze to the view from the aircraft window. As if relief from the physical distress of the hangover—and its murky psychological correlatives—was to be had from diverting his attention to the snowy mountainous vastnesses that crawl slowly past away beneath them!

Relihan now begins to imagine that normal terrestrial time has been abolished. And that this air journey is an unearthly interval between two contrasted aspects of his life. Between the infinite above and the sordidly finite beneath them, so he thinks to himself. He sees the clouds out there. Wisps of cotton wool, playthings of the stratospheric winds, pile up in gray masses over the high Siberian mountains to the south. Among them he sees elephants, sheep, dogs and angels plus the occasional monster. And away up there, the eternal limitless blue above the clouds, the silent inscrutable witness of Relihan's earthly achievements!

Or, was that vast empty space above really limitless?

Didn't he himself see a television program recently in which it was asserted that the universe was a vast sphere? Keep on going in a straight line from the point you are located presently, they said, and eventually you will reach your starting point. As certainly as certain can be! Maybe that "eventually" would mean thousands of millions of light years. Or millions of billions! But if this is the case, says Relihan to himself, of what does that nonexistence outside the charmed circle of reality consist? The whole thing is probably all a load of bullshit.

The taste of the bilious acid rising to his throat reminds them that such cosmic ponderings and speculative time travelling have never helped to cure a hangover. The very opposite, in fact! The hammer in his skull pounding away unceasingly bears out that insight. I had better change the script of these musings immediately or the silent passengers about me will have much more to complain about than a few lousy snores. Think positive, Relihan, he reminds himself!

Think of how you managed to reach Narita, Tokyo's main

airport, this morning, for example!

It was through pure luck that he had reached this flight on time, and well he knows it. He remembers, still a little fuzzily, that he woke up this morning in some hotel in Roppongi. At least, he thinks it was in Roppongi. But, to tell the God's honest truth, when he opens his eyes this morning he had no idea where he was or in what hotel he was sleeping. Except that he was somewhere in Tokyo, Japan!

And that he was fully dressed when he woke up, wearing his suit and his shoes, even, in bed. Always a bad sign! He couldn't even remember how he reached that particular hotel. Or where he was supposed to be going and doing today! He lay there in the semi-darkness, hoping that memory would throw some sort of lifeline in his direction. And, as luck would have it, it did just that.

One by one, the scattered fragments of yesterday came gradually into focus. Capped by the sudden, and exciting, realization that the object of his trip to Japan, that contract with Matsoka Cosmetech International, had been signed last night both by the President of Matsoka International and he himself in the multinational's headquarters in Harajuku.

That should surely give those Glenlongan begrudgers, whose numbers are not inconsiderable, some bitter cud to chew. Especially that bastard, Horan, who was against paying his travel and other expenses after the deal with Matsoka was done. Along with showing him and the other whingers that the son of old Dan Relihan was no lackadaisical pushover!

It wasn't for nothing that he named himself "The Glenlongan Tiger". Thanks to the good offices of his friends in the *Ballymore Herald*, a variant of that sobriquet, "The Tiger Relihan", had already secured a permanent niche for itself in the local folklore. To be followed by "The Glen Tiger – Conqueror of Japan", if he had anything to do with it! And a well-merited title it would be, by God, even if he had dreamt it up himself. Thirty five high-tech posts, for starters! And more to come, if the first phase of Matsoka Cosmetech's operation in Glenlongan enjoys the success the President of that company augurs for it.

And why wouldn't the venture be successful, with almost every Tom, Jack and Mary hell-bent these days on achieving a youthful appearance! And the demand for beauty and juvenescence technology increasing by leaps and bounds, accordingly, as the basis for the permanent prosperity of poor old Ireland is being laid by the Celtic Tiger Generation.

Yes sir, the politicians and the professors, the lads who know, are telling us that Ireland is on the glory path at last after centuries of misery, and that this path is leading us triumphantly into the foreseeable future. This is no country for old men, as some old poet or other was reputed to have said. The obese dream of recovering the svelte figures of their youth; old bags dream of transforming themselves into alluring young women. And Matsoka, in cahoots with Glenlongan Holdings, will be there in storied Glenlongan to help them realize their dreams. For a price!

Will he, Gus Relihan, have any chance of winning the annual Entrepreneur of the Year award? Why the hell not? He would have at least as good a chance as any other entrant in that lottery. He must find out if any judge of that competition is numbered among his acquaintances. A judicious well-placed word in a well-placed ear might work wonders.

And now, in his mind's eye, the *Taoiseach* is about to present him with that coveted annual award. Formal suits, dickie-bows and elegantly-gowned women! And Maura's eyes, bright with pride, adore him as he waits to take the stage. The applause is music in his ears already as he walks on the thick red carpet towards a smiling Taoiseach. Television cameras *whirr*. Damn it all, that dream is not the child of a superheated imagination; it is fucking-well feasible. He makes a mental note to mention the matter to his friend, the

Minister, as he passes through Dublin on his way to Glenlongan. If ever I can be of help to you, the same Minister said to him in the tent at Ballybrit, be sure to give me a shout...

But, fair play to those Japanese! Those lads, fair play to them, know how to give a successful business deal its merited social dimension. He lost count of the number of bars that those Matsoka executives and he himself had visited, and the number of taxis they had taken, after the Harajuku meeting. Drinking the health of the venture, and of each other, until the break of day, it seemed. They taught him how to say "*Kampai*". And he tried to teach them "Cheers" except that they seemed to know the word already, or some word like it that sounded like "Chills". So, as they raised their glasses and said "Chills" he responded with "Kampai" as everybody laughed.

A great night! The crack was mighty, even if there was no music. Great gulps of Sapporo beer interspersed with shots of Suntory whiskey! Whiskey mixed with beer is the very *divil* itself, as old Uncle Ned used to say. But worse than that was the saké, Japanese rice wine, for which he blames his memory loss. Not realizing the strength of this potion, he was gulping it back like water until he was warned by one of his hosts that saké is to be respected. In any case, he cannot remember how he reached this hotel, not to mention his room. Did his Japanese hosts escort him there to ensure he didn't go astray?

Lying comfortably there in the semidarkness, Relihan congratulates himself. In spite of the amount of drink he took on board last night, it appears to have had no effect on him. That's a miracle! A real miracle, surely! But a small weak voice speaks to him out of the experience of years.

Giving him to understand that the wages of sin have still to be earned, as he is still mildly pissed!

Jesus H. Christ!

Just as if he had a sudden vision of a monstrous tsunami rising up threateningly on the horizon of his calm sea, the next thought jars his consciousness. Pleasant lazy self-congratulatory thoughts are scattered like a flock of small birds at the sound of a shotgun. And Relihan leaps out of the bed with the celerity of a scalded cat, as he emits a long self-pitying groan. He turns on all the lights.

Mother of God! Am I not supposed to be in Narita Airport before 9:30 a.m., two hours before the departure time of the Moscow flight? Or so my printed schedule informed me.

And what the hell time is it now?

He knows that Narita is some distance out from the center of Tokyo. But he doesn't know if this hotel is on the airport side of the city. Or not! Jesus H. Christ! His watch informs him that it is almost 7:30 a.m. already. The hotel staff here must not have been informed about my flight time. There's not a single bloody second to spare. No time now for a shave, not to mention that long hot shower he had promised himself! He hurriedly bundles all the various personal items that are scattered around the room into his travel bag. That shower and a shave will have to wait until he reaches Moscow's Sheremetyevo Airport.

Ye Gods! If Natasha saw the cut of me now!

As he was pays his bill at reception, Relihan explains his predicament to the receptionist. The latter listens attentively to this departing guest, his features inscrutable. This will certainly not be the first, nor the last, time he has had to organize a rapid taxi transit to the airport. One more inebriated *gaijin* in danger of missing his flight!

I am afraid, sir, that there is no possibility that you will be able to make your flight in time, he says. The traffic between here and Narita is always very heavy at this time of day.

The problem is that I have an extremely important meeting in Moscow today, Relihan says quickly. If I miss my flight and that meeting, Japan stands to lose heavily. Your financial institutions could be badly damaged if I am not present there personally.

Hoping all the time against hope that his disheveled unshaven appearance and wrinkled suit will not give the lie to his story!

It is impossible to read from the features of the receptionist whether he believes Relihan's cock and bull story, or not. However, he accompanies the latter as they both walk rapidly to the head of the taxi rank outside the hotel. As he speaks, or rather barks, rapidly in Japanese to the small squat driver of the leading taxi he sounds like as if he is giving a military order. He then indicates wordlessly to Relihan, handing him a small card as he does so, that he take his place in the taxi in the seat beside the driver.

The taxi driver instantly puts his key in the ignition, the engine starts and the taxi shoots away from the rank with a tortured screeching of tires. Whatever instructions he had received from the hotel receptionist, this driver seems determined to break every traffic regulation known to the civilized world as his taxi roars through these Tokyo suburbs. The traffic is left in a mess behind them and Relihan prays that this mad race against time will not be spotted by some vigilant police officer. They break every single red light between Tokyo and Narita.

But now that the welfare of Japan is at stake: *Banzai!* It is just as well that I am half-cut, says Relihan to himself, or the deadly driving of this fuckin kamikaze would give me a heart attack.

He is the last passenger to board the Moscow flight. But even if his late arrival in the terminal delayed his flight departure by ten minutes, thus annoying the airport staff, as well as the other passengers—as can be seen clearly from their hostile glances cast in his direction—what if they knew that the financial stability and future wellbeing of Japan depended on my catching this flight? That would certainly change their tune. Although one would never know what they were thinking behind those impassive oriental faces. The important thing is that, against the odds, the Glenlongan Tiger is now aboard the Moscow flight! The Conqueror of Japan flyeth! And the contract with Matsoka International is secure in his travel case.

Relihan now looks down on the countryside over which they are flying. They have already left cloud-covered Vladivostok behind them, away down there, the seemingly interminable snow-covered mountain peaks and the deep desolate valleys of Siberia stretch southwards to the horizon. Glittering frozen rivers snake through the barren tundra towards the Arctic. Freezing cold, ice, darkness are images that Relihan associates with the barren wastes far below this luxurious capsule that flies over them. For all the world like some inhospitable distant planet. And as they fly over the occasional snowbound village he tries to imagine ordinary people down there, eating, drinking, working and fornicating. Lone trucks are as tiny insects crawling along with those long straight highways that link nowhere to nowhere. With a shudder, he seems to feel the chill of the grave rising up from the gloom of the gathering Siberian dusk as it gradually unfolds, in an unending panorama.

In other words, Gus Relihan does not feel that those images, spectacular though they be, are in any way conducive to a lightening of his spirit. The very opposite, in fact! He fears that as the tides of inebriation ebb, the spaces they vacate are going to be occupied by the mother of all hangovers, accelerated by such ruminations. So he channels his thoughts in what, it seems to him now, is a more promising direction. He now focuses on the delightful Natasha, that young Russian lady he will be meeting later in the Irish Pub in Sheremetyevo Airport.

Bringing the smooth marble thighs of Natasha into his imagination's focus may well serve to alleviate, even if ever so slightly, that murderous hangover that is now almost upon him. His wife, Maura, doesn't even suspect the existence of Natasha. Not to speak of her beauty, her youth, her figure or worse: her intuitive inventiveness in bed.

How could one compare Maura with Natasha? As a bedroom companion, for example? You must be bloody joking! The acts Maura would perform from a sense of duty, Natasha performs from raw desire. Relihan's wife knows, of course, that her husband stops off for a day or two in Moscow on his trips between Dublin and Tokyo. And hasn't she the option of displaying her gleaming *matrushkas*[23] and other lacquered Russian *tschotkes*[24] sitting on their mantelpiece in Glenlongan House as evidence of these brief stopovers and the global reach of her husband's ambitious forays.

And, being the most reasonable and understanding of women, she understands perfectly well that her husband needs such a respite after the meetings and sessions of hard bargaining in Tokyo. She appreciates that the tension and pressures that inevitably accompany her husband's bruising entrepreneurship, with the heavy responsibilities it entails, must be balanced by calm intervals of relaxation and reflection. Little does she suspect that the meaning she assigns to "relaxation" is at some remove from that of her beloved Gus.

Maura is a good mother, without the slightest shadow of doubt. Relihan cannot but admit that fact and sees no contradiction between this sincere appreciation and the satisfaction of those certain needs that inconveniently make themselves felt during her enforced absence. And, when all is said and done, he is inordinately proud of the children Maura presented him with. Isn't Ian already captain of his college's rugby team? And Jason is well on his way to becoming the leading swimmer in the county. He is bound to make the national Olympic team sometime in the near future, unless the demon drink gets its insidious claws into him.

[23] *A set of wooden dolls of decreasing size placed one inside the other.*
[24] *A small baubles or knick-knacks.*

As for the girls, Rosalind has taken her good looks from her mother, but she is far too given to the books. And writing bloody poems in Irish, for God's sake! But, given time and some fine young fellow, she'll get over all of that nonsense. Young Maura is his main cause for concern, however. He must think of some ruse to combat that medieval rubbish with which those damn nuns are filling her head...

And, as Relihan reminds himself, 10,000 meters above Siberia, why the hell should Maura even be aware of the existence of Natasha? Would an open confession to his spouse clear his conscience? Who in the name of Jaysus ever said that he had a conscience anyway! That is a fucking luxury I, Gus Relihan, can do without!

The Tiger understands full well that only the weak-minded, the weak and listless, find themselves troubled by a sense of guilt. Creeps with no backbone! Mindless jellyfish who allow themselves to be seduced by the thin voices of their ancestral ghosts instead of giving heed to the lusty voices of their own desires! He is reminded again of what that lecturer said at the business seminar he attended last year in Washington. Something about social conscience being an unnecessary weapon in the armory of the good folk chosen by destiny to conquer corporate heights. Greed is the one necessary modern virtue. All for one and one for one! Amen to that, says Relihan.

And, in any case, didn't he read somewhere recently that small adventures outside the matrimonial boundary were to be encouraged? Indeed, that such affairs may very well be necessary to save and reinvigorate floundering marriages. Some experts claim that extra-marital affairs can, and do, rescue marriages by releasing that poisonous tension that can build up between a couple in even the most sedate of marriages.

Neither does his Russian glamour girl, Natasha, know of the existence of Maura. Nor that same Maura has presented him with four beautiful offspring. Nor does Natasha know that Gus Relihan is already married. For, didn't he tell her that spring day in Red Square, just beside the Kremlin, in the shadow of whose brick-red walls the soot-dappled snow was melting, that he had never met the woman of his heart until just that moment? And that he had fallen in love with her, with Natasha, his budding Bolshoi ballerina.

In all fairness, it must be stated that Natasha is totally unaware of the existence of Relihan *per se*. For, Relihan revealed to her that his surname was Black. Yes, ma'am! Bob Black from Saskatchewan, an international freelance current affairs and business correspondent of Canadian nationality!

Natasha is certain that the pair of them will shortly marry. Life in Russia it is becoming increasingly desperate, she says. And she wants to escape from uncertainty about the future and the misery she sees all around her. Yes! She would abandon her beloved homeland for the sake of the children that she and "Bob Black" will have. (She fails to note the grimace that clouds Relihan's face momentarily as she passes that hot potato over to him). She wants them to settle in Vancouver. In a wooden house, near the ocean, she adds. With flowers in the garden! She had seen images of Vancouver in a travel documentary recently shown on Moscow TV. And the Canadian Embassy had sent on to her a batch of multicolored travel brochures featuring the delights of multicultural Vancouver ('Where Continents Meet'), its mild climate and its exotic Asian cuisine...

Relihan, wearing the mask of Bob Black, concurs and says that, coincidentally, he himself also had been thinking of settling in Vancouver. She reminds him then that Vancouver is not all that far from Saskatchewan. Relatively speaking! Or so she understands from the map the embassy sent her. So that it would be possible for them to make the occasional trip eastwards to visit his relatives who still farm there, the extended Black tribe.

But Relihan understands now that the time has come to put

an end to this lunatic pantomime. His affair with Natasha is far too dangerous a liaison to conduct in this global village. How the damn world has shrunk! You can find Irish tourists mooching around these days in the most unexpected places. Didn't he himself hear the dulcet tones of Gurrannabraher[25] ring out on the air in that vicinity of the basilica of St. Basil in Red Square, just as he was kissing Natasha? Not to mention that camera-bedecked Paddy, with his green leprechaun hat, who was staring at them as they strolled along, arm in arm, on the pathway beside the Moscow River. There do be ears on the walls in places where you would least expect it, Uncle Ned used to say. And, by God, how right that wise old codger was!

As he thinks about it, Relihan realizes that arranging a tryst in an Irish pub in Moscow was not the best idea ever. Jesus Christ almighty! If Maura ever got wind of the word, he would be landed fairly and squarely in the father and mother of all marital rows. Most importantly, his standing in the Glenlongan community would be irreversibly damaged. A blind eye might be cast on that sort of behavior in cosmopolitan Dublin. But in rural Glenlongan?

He opens his eyes as he detects people moving about him. Their blankets have been tossed off by most of the other passengers, some of whom have taken to walking up and down the aisle between the seats. There is a smell of food in the air and his morale perks up as he detects food and drink being served by air hostesses to the passengers at the top of the row of seats in which he is sitting. With some tasty morsels lining his stomach he would be better able to alleviate the symptoms of this monstrous hangover that are now moving to the center of his consciousness . With the help of a half pint of sake, of course! "A hair of the dog that bit you", Uncle Ned used to say, as he prescribed the only certain cure for a hangover that was sanctioned in the pharmacopeia of old Glenlongan.

---

[25]  *A working-class suburb of Cork City, Ireland.*

Relihan shuts his eyes again. Yes! He will make a decision. He most certainly will, before the dispensers of food and drink reach his seat. Yes, he is firmly resolved that he is going to end this "Wooing of Natasha by Bob Black" soap opera, for once and for all. Not this time though! Too late! The arrangement for this evening has already been made and, in the meantime, I have no way of getting into contact with Natasha.

The words of a Redemptorist priest, who delivered a sermon at a mission in Glenlongan in the bad old days, came unexpectedly to his mind. The binding rope of lechery is the most difficult rope to sever, said his reverence. But Gus Relihan is the man cut that rope, by God! Gus is no jellyfish now, and never was. He is nothing else but backbone. If there is a rope there for cutting, cutting is what he will do. The next time around, he will cut it. But, in the meantime...

Having made this momentous decision, Relihan now opens his eyes. Coinciding with the arrival of a food tray, handed to him by a smiling air hostess who, acceding to his request, also hands him—with a puzzled look—two small bottles of sake! It was just then he realizes, with a sickening jolt, that he is lacking his dentures.

How in the name of blazes was he going to eat those succulent pieces of sashimi there in front of him without a tooth in his mouth? Did he travel all the way from Tokyo in that condition? Obviously, he had. He must've been still too pissed up to now to notice that he was toothless. And if they weren't in his mouth, then where in the hell were those bloody teeth?

Gus Relihan is a creature of certain predictable habits, one of which is the placing of the dentures in his mouth every morning before rising. Every damn morning, without fail! But, this morning, thanks to the hurry and the confused state of his mind, he had neglected to perform that basic ritual. So, where were those dentures, then? A rapid search of his trouser pockets yielded not a single tooth. Likewise the pockets of his jacket! Now he was genuinely alarmed. Those damn teeth are not on his person, wherever they had hidden themselves.

Relax, Relihan, just take it easy! Don't let yourself get carried away! A calm measured voice, speaking to him from the back of his mind, advises him to take a deep breath and mentally backtrack, slowly and methodically, to enable him to identify the last moment he saw those teeth. C'mon, Relihan, your business training tells you that your problem, any problem, can be solved by the methodical application of common sense and strict rationality. So he assures himself.

Therefore, Relihan draws a deep breath of the stale cabin air into his lungs and sits back in his seat. The immediate problem is: without teeth, how is he going to eat that food in front of him?

He shuts his eyes and attempts to capture and retain images in his imagination images of last night's bacchanalia. Beads of cold sweat now stand out on his forehead. Far, in spite of his efforts to relax and image his last sighting of those dentures, they persist in playing hide and go seek with him, and his sense of frustration goes to the marrow of his bones.

It should be mentioned here that Mr. Gus Relihan is inordinately proud of his dentures. And why wouldn't he be? After all, he paid a pretty penny for them—$25,000 to be exact—in a dental clinic in Washington DC the week of the business seminar! He was pleased to pay that extortionate sum in the cause of personal vanity because these dentures could never be taken to be false teeth. Small irregularities in the positioning of the individual teeth, not common in artificial dentures, are among the features that create the illusion that they are fully natural.

So natural, indeed, that Natasha never guessed that her husband-to-be, Bob Black, was sporting artificial dentures. Indeed, she told him once that the scrupulous attention he paid to his dental care was what first attracted her to him. Unfortunately for us, she said, dental care does not appear to be a priority for the peoples of the new Russia, whose main concern is to get something to bite with our teeth rather than having them gleam. Maura told him that the magical American dentures take ten years, at least, off his actual age. Thanks to this observation, Relihan was able to inform Natasha (and what harm another tiny white lie on top of the heap he had already told her?) that he was almost 45 years of age, although he had celebrated his 57th birthday some months beforehand.

That is all very fine, Gus! But where in the hell were the same American dentures hiding on him now? Natasha would be beautifying herself in front of the mirror by this time, in all probability. Her delicate face, with those high Slavic cheekbones, slathered with some cream or other. Brushing her long fine blonde hair, she considers the image in the mirror of her imagination, that of the sparkling-toothed Bob Black, that warm hearted Canadian who is to be her life's companion—as well as their children's, of course—in a beautiful cottage with its flower garden beside the ocean in Vancouver. Probably humming to herself with self-satisfaction.

Relihan searches his pockets again, more carefully and methodically this time. With the same result. His pockets are as lacking in teeth as his own gums. If they are not in his pockets, is there a chance that they will be found in his travel-bag, down there somewhere in the darkness of the aircraft's hold? Highly unlikely! For, if he had got his hands on those dentures this morning, wouldn't he have thrust them into his mouth rather than into that travel bag?

As he digests that thought, Captain Nemoto announces that the aircraft will shortly be descending. And that all passengers should now return to their seats and fasten their safety belts. At that point exactly, an image with the aura of truth about it starts to emerge from the confused fog of Relihan's memories. He sees himself the previous night, just before he stretches himself out on the bed. And as the image come into sharper focus, he sees his dentures along with the signed copies of the contract with Matsoka International being placed carefully under a pillow in some hotel somewhere in Tokyo. The image is as clear as day. Somewhere in Tokyo, God help us...Under his pillow, so that they would be as safe as safe can be!

And that is where they still must be. Because it is absolutely certain that he did not look under that pillow as he packed his bag hurriedly this morning. Maybe, by this time, they have been thrown out by the cleaning staff? For, they are not likely to have been impressed by the parsimonious Mr. Relihan. Oh, why the hell didn't he remember to leave a decent tip on the table for them before vacating the room?

The Glenlongan Tiger sits there, horrified, as he considers the predicament that now faces him. What malign fate possessed him on that Kamikaze journey to Narita to tear into a million pieces the card that the hotel receptionist handed to him as they made for the taxi rank? And dump the results of this inopportune shredding into a rubbish container in the airport? That card would, doubtlessly, have given him the name and address of the hotel together with its phone number, the information he now so sorely needed. Because, without this knowledge, how the fuck is he ever going to locate that hotel again?

The loss of that signed contract with Matsoka doesn't even bear thinking about at this juncture! He can almost see the "I told you so" smirk on Mick Horan's greasy mug when the details of this unbearable episode come to light.

For, how the fuck is he ever going to find this document, or those dentures that are of the essence of the identity of Bob Black, in the Megalopolis that is Tokyo. Talk about needles in haystacks! They are only 10 minutes out from Sheremetyevo Airport, with the lights of Moscow below them, when the metallic voice of Capt. Nemoto makes an announcement. In God knows how many languages, one of which is possibly English. And, without a shadow of doubt, Natasha is waiting for him down there already in the Irish Pub. For the bright gleaming smile of Bob Black, the Canadian journalist who no longer exists...

Troubles seldom come singly, as Uncle Ned used to say! The captain now announces that he has an urgent message for Bob Black. This message startles toothless P.J. (Gus) Relihan. Nothing good will come of this, he mutters to himself. There is no such name on the passenger list, says the captain. And it seems to him that this message is written in some mysterious code. Would any passenger on this flight be in a position to help the crew to make sense of this message?

Relihan quickly makes up his mind. He rings his bell to draw the attention of the air hostess. It must be an urgent message from Natasha, since she opted to send it directly to the aircraft. He would invoke the powers of God and the devil, if needs be to ensure that she is not waiting in the bar, as they had planned, for the now nonexistent Bob Black.

The hostess hurries down the aisle towards him. Relihan tells her that he is certain that the message is for him. She looks at him somewhat doubtfully. At his toothless mouth, his unshaven jaws and his bleary eyes! She checks the number of his seat against the passenger list in her hand.

But aren't you P.J. Relihan?, she asks.

Exactly, he says. I am the man in question. "Bob Black" is a pseudonym I use occasionally for theatrical purposes. Some people know me by that name only.

Have you any evidence of that on paper?

I am afraid not! I am not on an acting tour this time around.

Well then, I'll have to consult with the captain to see if he will allow you to see the message.

And she leaves him, walking back up the aisle between the passenger seats. She shuts the pilot's cabin door behind her. Relihan briefly considers the complexity of Japanese bureaucracy. The inexplicable difficulties that appear to attend the simplest matters! The rigidity that refuses to allow exceptions! The long labyrinthine discussions before the making of a decision!

The disagreeable sensation in his eardrums lets him know that the aircraft is descending. Looking out of the window again, the lights of Moscow tilt as they turn once again, they being one of a number of planes stacked up over the airport awaiting permission to land. The voice of the captain is heard again as he informs the passengers that the temperature of Sheremetyevo is a cool -17 C and that snow storms are forecast for the Moscow region. Relihan hears the clunk of the landing-gear as it is lowered and wonders what the hell is keeping the air hostess.

Is he fated to never know the content of that message for Bob Black? What could Natasha have been attempting to communicate to him? Hopefully, she is trying to inform him that she cannot meet him at the place and time appointed. Because, dear Natasha, without his American dentures, Bob Black has ceased to exist! Your lover, that Canadian journalist from Saskatchewan you have chosen to be the father of your children, has vanished.

Just as his impatience and curiosity is about to impel P.J. (Gus) Relihan is about to press the help button in order to draw the cabin staff's attention, the door of the crew's cabin opens. And, once again, the same hostess walks down the aisle towards him, swaying as she does so with the movement of the aircraft, and carrying a tray this time. She stops beside Relihan. There is a piece of paper on the tray.

The captain says that you are allowed to read this message. But since we have no definite proof that you are the Bob Black to whom it is addressed, we cannot allow you to keep it.

A Japanese solution for a non-Japanese problem! The air hostess extends the tray towards him. He looks sharply at the piece of paper. This is no code, by God. It is simply a short sharp message in the Irish language. It says:

*Stay with your Russian slut, you bastard!*

*Maura (your soon-to-be ex-wife)*

# ABOUT THE AUTHOR

Tomás Mac Síomóin is an award-winning Gaelic novelist, storyteller, poet, and journalist. A doctoral graduate of Cornell University, he has lived in Catalonia since 1998. Translations from, and into, Spanish and Catalan, including Juan Rulfo's *Pedro Páramo* and the poetry of Ernesto Cardinal, figure among his work, along with polemical essays of cultural and political analysis.

His poetry has been translated into many European languages, most recently Slovenian and Rumanian. His short story *Music in the Bone* has been selected by The Dalkey Archive Press for inclusion in *Best European Fiction 2013*. An English-language translation based on his award-winning novel *An Tionscadal* is due to be published in 2013 by Nuascéalta Teoranta.

Made in the USA
Middletown, DE
22 September 2022

11033966R00119